THE MULEY HEAD STRANGLER

A Final Squeeze Just To Please

Sybil Darlette

PREFACE
THE MULEY HEAD STRANGLER

"Now, ain tryin' to steal nothin' from nobaddy. Ain beatin' up old folks. Ain't even touched Clara Matty, and she knows she is askin' fudd. Om jess tryin' to make my livin' the best way that's right for me. My brudda just finished a 18-month stay in the county jail for a lie some 'ho told the police. So for now, he stayin' wit me in my apoddment. I guess that's good cos I could use some baddy to help me out right now. It ain't too easy recovering from an abortion when the mane tryin' to hold ya down by not givin' ya proper medical cure just cuz you caint prove an income. That's funny though, cuz on Friday nights after dey leave dey fancy offices and befo dey go home to dey wives and girlfriends and life partners, dey manage to stop by Spicey's Hangout. I make dey forty-hour work week worth it. My pocket gets at least twenty-five percent of the money from foreign bank accounts nobaddy know 'bout, but me. Ya see, Im the chocolate sista on dey um, and in dey beds when dey have island poddys to impress yacht club membas. Dockta Jacob Ronnie himself treated me in his private office after I told 'em there was mix up at the bar. His ass had tha nerve to tell me go take care of it, like I gots some kinda Beverly Hills Health Insurance.

You shoulda seen how quick he got me in dat office when I refreshed his memory about a private poddy in the back of the Hangout. Now for me, the pay was worth it, but my fee did not include possible abortions, so either he had to buy my personal health insurance or take chances. Well, old Jacob Ronnie got a little too full and said let the chips fall where they may. Hmp, I guess he hadn't realized one of those chips had fallen in me. Ya see, news of my abortion had managed to spread throughout da neighborhood, especially among my rival working girls. They figured the condition would slow me down and eventually put me outta bitness. That was dumb. Did they really expect for my main line of work in supporting myself to shut down? Sure dey did, but dey amateurs. Imma pro. I gots finances sat aside to cover dis hide."

Contents

MINE YO BITNESS

Stank Stank was laying on the couch wearing nothing but a pair of black and gray striped boxer briefs. The thin sheet partially covering him from the knee down, was hanging to the floor. His left hand was inside the top band of his boxers as he mumbled something incoherent. Spicey walked in holding a weekly planner.

"Stank, you gotta get up and go check the bah for me." She told him. Stank Stank rolled over and fell off the couch, waking up immediately.

"Damn! Shit!" He yelled. He looked up and saw Spicey standing over him. "What up lil sis?" He asked, yawning. "Why you ain't tell me I was fallin?"

"Boy, you crazy." She told him. "For real though, I need you to run by my ba and check thangs out for me. See if my gurls been making any money in the back."

"I gotcha lil sis. Besides, Mrs. Matty want s me to stop by and put some stuff in da attic ful." He said. Standing up and stretching, he added," knowing Mrs. Matty, she probably just wanna know how you doin'."

"Stank you ain't spreadin' my bitness ish ya?" Spicey asked, smirking.

"Nawl gurl. You know I aint tellin' nothin' but how my lil sussa got all rich selling alcohol and thangs to ole rich white men." He winked at her and picked up yesterday's stained, dusty jeans and slipped into them. "Just tell me why you gotta cater to the old ones? Damn!" He wrinkled his face and shook his head.

Spicey pulled a skinny cigar out of her robe pocket and lit it. Widening her eyes and giving Stank Stank her serious look, she answered, "Damn boy, don't you know nothin'?

Dey the ones who got them mature bank accounts. Mo money, mane.

She reached into the other pocket and pulled out a set of keys attached to a huge fake diamond ring. "You run my gas out, put it back in." She told him,' I know you goin' showcasing."

"You know om good fud." He replied, while grabbing the keys and rushing towards the candy apple red sports coupe.

Tossing him a red muscle shirt to match his cap, she hollered, "Boy, put a shirt on! You handlin' bitness. Look professional! Tie yo' shoes up!"

Backing out of the parking space, Stank Stank smiled, at her, just as the sun and mirror reflected off his gold tooth. It sent a strong bright glare into Spicey's eyes. She shook her head. "Heesa fool, but dats my boy,." She said, as she closed the door smiling.

Stank Stank took the long way to the bar. He turned on the radar detector and raced down the highway at a cool hundred fifteen miles per hour, taking the exit to the bar in a good eight minutes flat. Just as he slowed his roll, for the off off-ramp, the detector picked up a radar.

"Fuk!" He said to himself. There was an unmarked squad car parked behind Spicey's bar. Fearing the possibility of a raid, he quickly circled the building and phoned his sister.

"Yo Sussa. Why popo out back?" He asked her.

"That's Cloggsdale Longstreet. The mayor of Myron County." She informed him. "He's a regular."

"He sho enjoyin' hisself'." Stank Stank told her." He aint seed me yet."

He passed by the car again and saw someone wearing a pink wig in the front seat. "Who wearin' dat pink hure?" He asked inquisitively. "Ole girl workin' hawd."

Spicey giggled. "Is that so? I guess the place is still making money, even with me out sick. The girl with the pink hair is Sexie." She told him.

"Yeah, well, I caint see all dat." Stank Stank replied. "I'll take ya word fudd, cuz ole boy still don't know I exist."

He parked the car near the driveway just as EasySlide pulled into the lot in his old 1987 convertible with fading paint and 24-inch tires. Stank Stank blew the horn and threw up a deuce sign. EasySlide got out of the car holding a bottle concealed in a brown paper bag.

Slamming the heavy car door, he quickly scanned the parking lot before walking over to greet Stank Stank.

"What up mane! What you doin' hure, dawg?" He asked. "I thought you'd be layin' low right now."

"Just checkin' thangs out for Spicey." Stank Stank answered. "Glad to see you support my girl though."

They walked to the door and entered the darkened bar.

"Ain't no thang." Easyslide told him. "Hell, I enjoys comin' hure. Ev-va time I walk in, nigga feelin' like Sanna Claws." He pointed out two employees barely dressed in enough clothes to be seen in public. "Ho, ho and ahhh', he laughed wickedly and grabbed at his goatee when he saw a thick voluptuous woman in a pair of tight brown leggings walking by, 'ho." He said and winked at her.

"Yo mama a ho." She told him as she walked by.

"All baby, it aint like dat baby. See, a mane like me will take a woman like you home to meet mama." He lied, following behind her.

"Look hure gurl, what yo name is anyway?" He asked. She turned around and gave him a blank stare.

"Hundud Dollas." She answered.

Easyslide slowly backed away towards the mens' room.

"I be back baby. You gone wait for me?" He replied and joined Stank Stank at the bar.

"You gone hit dat?" Stank Stank asked, after downing a shot of whiskey.

"Beer on Tap!" EasySlide called out to Dope, the bartender. "Hell nawl!" He answered. "Dat bitch wont a hundud damn dollas. Sheen all dat. Gat damn purple ass weaves all up in her head and shit. Tryna act like she da hot sauce on my nake bones. Hell nawl. I aint da one!" He mouthed.

Stank Stank lit a cigarette and looked around the room. "Yeah, mane." He told him."

Sometimes it beez like dat. I tell ya sump'um though. Watch yo back cuz dem rich ass white boys love dem some Mercedes."

Easyslide gulped down the mug of beer and let out a loud, long belch. "Damn, dat was some good burr." He said.

"So you jess come hure to see da ho's?" Stank Stank asked. He inhaled the cigarette smoke and slowly made rings in the air. EasySlide looked at him and laughed. "Mane, who you s'pose da be? Sum Lil nigga givin' out smoke signals?"

They stopped talking when a short lady with an outrageously plump rear came from the back room. Stank Stank nearly choked on the smoke he'd just inhaled.

"Damn!" He managed to say, through a fit of coughing.

"Damn ain't da werd." EasySlide said, pointing towards the lady. "Dat dare why I come hure ev'ra chance I get. Me and Fo-five gats some bitness to handle."

"Dat her name, height, or price?" Stank Stank asked, crushing out the cigarette butt.

"She go by Fo-five." EasySlide responded. "But wit a azz like dat, who da hell cure!" He slapped Stank Stank on the back. "Know-what-I-mean playa?" He spun around on the bar stool. "See that gal over thurr wit the pink hure?"

"Yeah, dat's Sexie." Stank Stank said.

"Sho ya right." EasySlide replied. "Dat's Fo- five's cousin, ya see, she be ackin' all like she wonts her somma dis!" He shared. "I might have ta get myself into some dubba trubba.

Shee-it. If a brudda like me can get some play hure', he clapped and rubbed his hands together devilishly, ' then it's on like pop cone."

The girls were working hard, preparing to open for business. It was almost six and they still had to sweep the floor, clean the backrooms, and wipe down the poles. There was a loud   tap on the door and Stank Stank looked at his watch. It was a little after five.

Spicey had told him what time to expect the security guards, so he called one of the girls to open the door. Up until five, the only male that usually hung around the place was Dope, the bartender. Spicey would ask him to come in early sometimes just to have a male presence there, with the girls, until the guards arrived.

The door opened and in walked a towering 6'8 of a man, looking like he didn't weigh any less than three hundred and fifty pounds. He ducked his head a little when he entered and walked straight up to Stank Stank. Stank Stank got off the bar stool, preparing for confrontation, while EasySlide slowly made his way behind the bar area for a few empty bottles, just in case. The giant of a man extended his hand to Stank Stank and tilted his midnight black sunglasses down. "My nigga!" He said and smiled.

"I know you, poddna?" Stank Stank asked, shaking the man's hand.

"Mane, ev'ra mulfucka from here to wes of Mrs. Sippi know yo' ass." He said.

EasySlide finally came from behind the bar when he saw the bartender come from the restroom. Stank Stank checked the notes Spicey had given him.

"James Gruesome!" He said. " What up mane?".

"Protectin' 'hos and openin' doughs." He said. "How lil momma doin'?" "She good." Stank Stank told him.

"Show be good to see her back." Gruesome responded respectfully, as he excused himself and walked towards his spot at the door.

"Yo ass still famous 'round hure. Damn!" Easy Slide commented. "You know, Punky werk hure too don'tcha?"

"Who da hell iz Punky?" Stank Stank questioned.

"Ree-Ree's brother," Easyslide answered. "You remember hur lil punk ass brother LoShun? ReeRee from tenth tenth-grade mane. She had dem bic thick ass glasses and was poplar wit

the basketball team." Stank Stank smiled and thought about the days when he played a little ball in high school. He slapped hands with Easy Slide for a while like two little boys.

"Mane Ree-Ree wudn't no joke. Come Friday night after dem dances, Spike that punch and she was the life of the poddy for ev'body. "Stank Stank remembered. " Two, three niggaz later and she still goin'. Ree-Ree wuz a lil cray cray wit da drank drank".

Stank Stank wrinkled his forehead and looked at the ceiling for a few seconds.

"The only brother she had was dat lil weak ass bastard, who ended up dropping out of high school and joining the military." Stank Stank recalled.

"Yeah, well, heen weak no mo." Easy Slide told him. "I seed my boy put down a kickboxer. Had em screaming like a lil bitch right ova thure on da flo . Gurls laughing at em and shit. "

"Dis Spicey's Place." Stank Stank said proudly. "Sheen havin' no stuff here."

Stank Stank turned to EasySlide with seriously wide wide-open eyes.

"Look hure mane, I gotta run and take ole Mrs. Matty to the place to get some commodities and thangs. You gonna be 'roun awhile?" He questioned.

"You straight hure. Jess let J.T. know. He always gots ha back." Easy Slide said while eyeing Fo-five. " I needs to come back later tonight wit a flat fitty myself. Take cure of bitness and buy a couple dranks afterwards."

EasySlide smiled and bumped Stank Stank on the shoulder with his fist.

Making eye contact with Gruesome, Stank Stank met up with him at the door. Stank Stank explained things while Gruesome smiled and nodded like a trained little puppy.

The whites of his eyes glowed like a full moon in the darkened sky. Stank Stank shook his hand and slipped him a C-note.

"My nigga!" Gruesome said again, as he stood close to Stank Stank, displaying his one crooked, chipped tooth. He took an ancient-looking phone from a pouch on his belt and took a selfie with Stank Stank. Stank Stank eyed the girls one last time while smacking his mouth and sucking in on his bottom lip. He tilted his head at EasySlide when he got his attention and Easy Slide ran over to him.

"Gotta roll mane." Stank Stank announced, while fist bumping him. " Momma Matty waiting on me." EasySlide was busy eyeing Fo-Five, but managed to give his buddy a quick head nodd.

Gruesome smiled admirably at Stank Stank.

"My nigga!" He announced once more. His white teeth glowed perfectly through his wide smile, under the dim neon lights. Stank Stank, feeling like playing big shot, handed him an extra rolled up fifty.

"Watch da place for me mane." He told him. "I got thangs to do."

"Nuttin' but a werd dawg." Gruesome told him, while rubbing the unknown bill between his fingers and nodding. Stank Stank smiled and ran out the door to the car. Once inside, he celebrated his fame.

"Now dat's what om tawkin' 'bout." Stank Stank whispered to himself. "Respect a nigga!" He lit an apple apple-flavored cigar and pulled out the driveway heading towards the old Mom and Pop Grocery Store and Car Wash. Gruesome watched, smiling, from the door of the bar.

Stank Stank was feeling like a million dollars as he drove along singing with the radio.

"Big bootys say uh-uh, big bootys say uh. Clap it, smack it, wiggle it too.

Twerk it, werk it, you know what to do. Big bootys say uh-uh, big bootys say uh Big bootys say uh-uh, big bootys say uh Clamin' dat pole, doin' it rite

Makin' it rain all through the nite, Grabbin' dat dough, high and low, Bouncin' dat booty up off the flo

Big bootys say uh-uh, big bootys

say uh Big bootys say uh-uh, big bootys say uh."

At the next exit, he pulled onto the parking lot of a small mom and pop store and stopped   in front of the dumpster. He took a small plastic bag from the glove box and started filling   it with trash and garbage from the car. He was making sure to collect all torn wrappers and used items from under the seats, besides the passenger door and anywhere else Ms. Matty may happen to accidentally look while inspecting a vehicle she'd never seen before. Taking a quick break from car cleaning, he stood up and began to bust a few moves. Spreading his legs apart and bending them at the knees, he balled his fist up and started pointing towards the trash bin as if he was fussing at it. He tucked his lower lip under his front teeth and frowned his face like he was sniffing all the garbage in the container. He stiffened his neck and moved his head back and forth like an angry chicken before repositioning his pants upon his waist and swinging his arms like he was doing some kind of short quick judo chops.

"Ain nobody payin' you

To do a dance you cain't do. Spread dem cheeks, Drop it deep.

Hit the flo with dem peaks.

Om say'n big bootys say uh-uh-uh Big bootys say uh. Om say'n big bootys say uh-uh-uh

Big bootys say uh.

He jumped back in the drivers' seat and turned the car around so fast and hard that it left tire marks on the pavement and frightened bystanders.

Pulling out of the driveway, he made a swift right turn and entered the highway speeding to Mrs. Matty's house.

Back at the bar, Fo-Five came sashaying past Punky and jumped onto the circular stage. She wrapped one leg around the pole and positioned her hands a little higher, inner-locking her fingers. She began to gyrate wildly while throwing her head backwards. Slowly and erotically, she began humping the pole to the beat of the sultry jazz music.

"Make it clap and I'll make it rain." Punky yelled out to her. He held up a small stack of ones and waved them in the air. Fo-Five smiled at him, displaying the full length of her tongue in what was supposed to have been a sexy, flirtatious, type of laugh. Dropping it like it was hot, she shook her nearly exposed rear just inches above the floor, taking all eyes off her red lace stilettos.

"You aint s'pose to be watchin' me reherz." She teased playfully. "Yo job is to watch tha folks coming in to see all dis." She explained, rubbing her hands over her body as if she was enticing him with some tasty treat.

Punky held his head back, tossed a few peanuts into his mouth and smirked. "Dayne hure yet." He replied.

Ooo Wee walked past the bar bouncing her nearly naked backside, flirtatiously, at Dope.

Dope let out a long loud whistle. "Ooo Wee!" He yelled. " Momma, why caint dat booty be free?"

She smiled and laughed at him while sticking her tongue so far out of her mouth that it looked unreal. "Gone now Dope." She said. "You know you caint handle me."

Just then, Sexie came running from one of the back rooms with a sheet draped over her naked body. She was looking around hastily for Gruesome. She had some alarming news for him. Gruesome saw the fear in her face and immediately clenched his fist and prepared for action, while walking towards her with the harsh look of threat and intimidation showing in his eyes.

"J. T. Why all dem polease cahhs out back." She asked. "We gettin' raided au something?" Unaware of the situation, Gruesome rushed to the back window to check things out.

"Oh my damn!" He growled. Jumping over tables and hurling towards the back, he watched curiously as several blue shirts walked around an unmarked squad vehicle. One officer circled the car with yellow tape while a short, fat guy with a rugged beard and overlapping belly, took pictures.

Right there in view of everyone on the inside, Sexie unrolled a pair of underwear from her hand and tried to put them on as discreetly as possible while keeping the thin sheet over her body.

"I gotta get outta hure J.T.', she said, 'I didn't take dis job looking for trouble."

"Take it easy, baby girl." He told her. "Dis may not have nuttin' to do wit you." Dope removed a case of dental floss from his pocket and tore off a twelve twelve-inch strand.

"What you say 'bout it boss?" He asked Gruesome, while dangling part of the flavored string from his mouth.

"Caint say right now."" Gruesome said, still peeking out the window.

"That cah been there since yesterday. I remember seeing it." Dope told Gruesome. "You think it's stolen?" He asked.

"Iown know right now, Dope." He said quietly. His deep voice resembled the growl of a mild mannered grizzly bear.

"Dat's dude's cau." Punky said. "The weird dude. He one of Spicey's regulars from across county line." Punky paused in thought. "I sho hope he aw ight."

Everyone watched the action outside as more and more cop cars arrived. Inside, Sexie was dripping with sweat so badly that she dropped the sheet that she had covering her body while trying to put on a bra. It fell completely to the floor. Dope got a good and up close view of her plump, round breast and darkened nipples. He licked his thin lips, winked and motioned her to the backroom with his head.

"Long as dey don't cawl the meat wagon, we good." Gruesome told them. Just then, the white van pulled onto the scene. Gruesome removed the old old-style flip phone from his hip pocket case and phoned Stank Stank. One thing they didn't need was a dead white

man, in an unmarked squad car, outside a brothel ran by a high class ebony pimptress. Before pushing the fast dial number, he bellowed out a few orders.

"Ya'll lock dem doughs. We gon be closed da day, look like. All of yall, get dressed. Dey may be coming in hure to ask qurtions." He picked up a napkin and wiped the perspiration from his bald head and turned to Dope.

"Mane, fix me a strong one. Ain feelin' dis shit at all." He said.

"Rum, whisky or bourbon?" Dope asked. He reached for the nearby stainless steel shaker.

"Whisky." Gruesome responded. His eyes were still glued on the action out back. "Make me one of dem sayz-rag cottales."

Dope flipped the shaker in the air and grabbed a short, round glass. "One sazerac cocktail coming up." He said.

Miles away, Stank Stank took the first exit off the highway onto Recreation Road. This way, he could cruise through Gilleylen State Park and show off Spicey's car. Especially, if he spotted some of his buddies out drinking and smoking. He slowed his speed and glanced over by the huge historic oak tree, where he and his posse used to hang out after school to enjoy a few rounds of Mary Jane when he was growing up. He momentarily removed his hands from the steering wheel to light a cigarette. When he passed the posted 15 miles per hour speed limit sign, he lowered the drivers' side window to let the smoke out and spotted flashing red and blue lights in the rear-view mirror. While slowing to a stop, he heard a lady's voice coming through a megaphone.

"You see deez lights!" The officer yelled. "Pull over!"

Stank Stank pulled over to the side of the two-way street, the best he could, without parking on the grass. He turned the key to the off position and waited patiently. He wondered what he did to attract this kind of attention. Either way, he didn't want to make matters worse, so he decided to cooperate with the little lady. Opening the door of the squad car and kneeling behind it, the officer yelled, "Get out of the car and keep your hands where I can see them!" Stank Stank slowly and carefully opened the door of the car and stepped out with his hands above his head. When he turned to face the officer, he saw the barrel of a sawed sawed-off shotgun aimed straight at him.

"Aw damn!" He thought, dropping the cigarette from his mouth and keeping his hands up. The officer stood up and returned the gun to it's holster while staying prepared to draw at any moment. With his chest stuck out, all bad and tough looking, he approached Stank Stank.

"What's your name boy?" He asked, while trying to sound as manly as possible. It was at this moment that Stank Stank realized that the officer wasn't a lady, but a short, stocky framed man with a high pitched voice. Stank Stank smirked at the officer's youthful, female sound.

"It sho da hell ain't boy." He accidentally said out loud..

"Oh! You're one of them!" The officer responded. He spit some brown liquid upon the clean pavement and wiped his mouth on his hairy freckled arm, while repositioning a lump in his cheek. He walked over and snatched Stank Stank around in one hard, swift motion and placed him in handcuffs. Turning him back around by poking him in the shoulder with his Billy club, the officer removed his mirrored sunglasses displaying his cold, hazel eyes

and gave Stank Stank a stern look. This was supposed to have delivered a threat of bodily harm, so Stank Stank looked straight into his bloodthirsty eyes and answered.

"Mawcell Robinson, sur." The officer took a few steps back and replaced his sunglasses.

"Pruddy nice car you got here, Mr. Robinson." The officer said. "I sure cain't afford nothing like this on my salary." He wipped his nose. "But chew can huh?"

"It aint mine sur." Stank Stank confessed. "It's my sussa's".

"Your sister's huh?" The officer questioned.

"You got some identification." He asked curiously.

"Fo Sho! It's in my back pocket, on the right side." Stank Stank directed.

The officer reached in Stank Stank's pocket and removed his wallet. He glared intensely at the valid drivers' license, trying to find fault with it.

"Sez here, you're Mawcell Robinson alright." He admitted, somewhat disappointedly. He stood there momentarily and starred at Stank Stank.

"The name Robinson reminds me of a business partner of mine." He said, and smiled. "Good ole Spicey. That's one hot ass gal who knows how to give a real good pardy." He remembered.

He glanced back at his cruiser as he went through Stank Stank's wallet.

"Only twelve dollas on ya? Well, hell, you cain't be related to Spicey. You aint got no money boy." He said, trying to intimidate Stank Stank.

"Call me boy one 'mo gen." Stank Stank whispered.

The officier tugged at his radio, preparing to call in Stank Stank's license number.

"Spicey my susta." Stank Stank blurted out.

The officer looked at him in surprise. "You're Spicey Robinson's brother?" He asked. "The young lady who runs the bar and grille a few miles up the road?"

Stank Stank nodded. "Yea mane."

The officer quickly turned Stank Stank around and removed the handcuffs and offered up an explanation.

"You see, Mr. Robinson, there was a mugging at the store a few miles up the road and the guy got away with old Ms. Millie's pocketbook. We are just trying to cover all corners.

Youknow how it is, don't you?" He said. He glanced through Spicey's car one last time.

"You have a good day now, Mr. Robinson, ya hear?" He said, while getting back in the squad car. He forced a smile and waved at Stank Stank as he drove by.

Stank Stank drove off behind him. "Damn Spicey!" He said. "You sho nuff got it goin' on!

WHO DO YOU SEE?

Look at me!

Tell me.

What you see.?

Do you see a person of interest,

an ex-con, or a gangsta wannabe?

Maybe you see a man who should no longer be free.

Someone who needs to be chained up, caged, beaten,

or hung from a tree.

Perhaps a man with criminal compulsions, hmmm?

You think that's me?

Look at me now . (turns to side profile and covers head
with a dark hoodie and dons a pair of sunglasses).

Tell me,

Who do you see?

Am I the guy who robbed you blind,

and stole your daughter's virginity? (gyrates hips in a
circular motion)

Ha! Sucka! (turn and look straight ahead, removes
sunglasses and folds arms)

You think that's me?

Go on, slam me to the ground, arrest me,

Do what you will. (removes hoodie)

Refuse my suggestion to chill.

Feed my thoughts to kill

YOU!

For an injustice that's so surreal

To you, I'm just another person offered a plea deal.

Am I Jack or am I Jill?

Six months in,

I won't know what's real.

Hump! I want my revenge upon you still.

A mile and a half later, Stank Stank was turning onto Mrs. Matty's street. He reached down to adjust the volume on the radio and spotted Spicey bent over into a car.

Her thin white booty shorts were doing their job of showing off her lime green polka dot hip hip-huggers, that matched her low- cut crop top. Stank Stank honked the horn as he passed by. Six houses later when he turned into Mrs. Matty's driveway, his phone slid forward. He reached down to retrieve it and realized the battery was dead. He winced and jumped out of the car. Through the picture window, he could see old old-time photos hanging on Mrs. Matty's walls as he approached the door. He pulled on the handle and called out to her.

"Mrs. Matty Om hure." He yelled. "You in dare?"

"Okay baby. Om commin'. " The old lady responded. "Ain 'specta see you taday after what happened at yo sussa's bitness." She informed him. Stank Stank glared at her suspiciously. "What you mean Mrs. Matty?" He asked.

She waved him into the kitchen where she set sat with her 12" color tv.

"Sey dey found a dead white mane behind Spicey's ho house." She told him while pointing at the Special News Report. Stank Stank's eyes popped open as wide as silver dollars.

"Mrs. Matty, you got somewhere I can plug in my phone." He asked, while pulling a charger cord from his pocket. She pointed at the wall behind the tv.

"Rat ova there." She pointed.

"Mane, I gotta call Spicey." Stank Stank said excitedly, while dialing her number.

"Mane, mane, mane, mane, mane, mane!" He repeated, while jumping up and down on his tiptoes.

"Om sorry, Mrs. Matty, I gotta piss." He said, while holding his "junk."

"Well gone in thell boy. Grabbing it witcho hane ain't gonna keep it in." She told him.

Stank Stank ran around the corner and into the bathroom, not bothering to close the door.

With his free hand, he re-dialed Spicey's number but his phone was dead. When he returned to the kitchen, he connected the power cord and checked his phone. He saw several missed calls from J.T. Gruesome and one recorded message marked URGENT.

As he recalled, Gruesome was the main security guard at the bar. He needed to contact Spicey as soon as possible.

"Spicey right down the skreetskreet, Mrs. Matty. Come on. "We gone go get hur and drop you off at the center for yo commodities. We'll swing by and grab you afta we check thangs out." He told her. Mrs. Matty grabbed her purse and followed Stank Stank to the living room door, where they were stopped by Spicey, who was about to enter.

"Hey old lady." Spicey greeted, as Stank Stank opened the door. "Hey Ho." Mrs. Matty responded.

"I got yo ho." Spicey shot back.

"I know you do." Mrs. Matty responded. "Rat twinx ya laids." "We gotta roll ya'll." Stank Stank intervened.

He looked at Spicey with seriously wide eyes and explained. "Dey done found a dead white mane in a cahh behind the hangout."

Spicey immediately started patting her pockets and digging in her bra for her phone. "Damn it!" She shouted, while getting in the back seat. "I must've left my phone at the fuckin' condo! I need to know who they found." She yelled. Stank Stank glanced at her for using such a harsh word with Mrs. Matty present.

"Dey sey his name Loneskreet or sump'n like dat." Mrs. Matty informed. She looked at Spicy who had her mouth closed for a change. To her surprise, Mrs. Matty saw tears beginning to build up in Spicey's eyes as she continued. "Said dat he was a male, over in Mile-run County." Mrs. Matty dug deep into her large purse and pulled out a block of tobacco. She broke off a piece and secretly put it in her mouth and began to chew steadily.

"Dead ol rich white mane, behind a ho house, run by a young black ho, um um, she said as she nodded her head, you gonna need a lawyer baby." She advised.

Spicey was so quiet, in the back seat, that the silence along tugged at Mrs. Matty's heart. "Mrs. Matty sho sorry." She empathized. "Was he yo John?"

Spicey just wasn't feeling like arguing, so she ignored the last part of the old lady's statement. "Cloggsdale Longskreet was one of my best customers." She said through sniffles.

"Mrs. Matty sho nuff sorry to hear dat," she said, while nudging Stank Stank on the arm. "You gone and go to her bitness, Poo. Mrs. Matty can get dem commodities any ole time."

She looked back at spicey and gave her a tissue from her purse.

"It'll be alright." She told Spicey. "You find another rich ole mane to jump up and down on ya real soon. You see."

Stank Stank went back through the park and made it to Spicey's bar in record time. He turned into the driveway and swooped the car around back, leaving nothing but a trail of dusk behind him. Punky was on his way out of the bar, but immediately went back inside to alert Gruesome of Stank Stank's arrival. When he stopped the car,

Punky and Gruesome came running towards him with news of the incident. Spicey stepped out of the backseat and quickly looked over the scene. While Punky filled Stank Stank in with all the details, Gruesome held Spicey closely, comforting her, as he confirmed the suspicion.

"Sorry lil momma. It was Cloggsdale Longskreet." He told her. "Somebaddy done kilt him." Spicey held onto Gruesome as if she was frozen. Then she turned around and pounded her hands into the top of the car.

"Fuck!" She screamed.

Mrs. Matty jumped a little, accidentally expelling juices from her cheek onto the dashboard of the car. Prying her right hand from the armrest, she got a black cloth from her purse and quickly wiped down the car's interior, before opening the door and stepping out.

"You aw'ight Mrs. Matty?" Stank Stank asked.

"Yeah baby. Mrs. Matty just fine." She answered, as she made her way toward the wooded area to spit. Looking back at Stank Stank, she could see Punky making all kinds of weird hand and arm gestures as he laid out the entire scene.

"Need ya to call it Boss Lady." Gruesome whispered to Spicey. "Do we open fa bitness taday?" Spicey Looked at Gruesome and paused for a second. Her face was covered with tears.

"He was one of my best customers. He paid well. I thought ev'rybaddy loved him." She cried. Gruesome removed a bar napkin from his back pocket and gave it to her. Spicey cleaned her face and cleared her throat before giving orders.

"Have the girls dedicate a show to him. We caint make money if we closed." She told him.

Mrs. Matty walked the area like she was a licensed detective. She picked up several discarded objects from the ground and placed them in a plastic sandwich bag. She pulled a small pair of binoculars from her purse and looked at the top of trees. She counted footsteps from the trees to the back door of the bar and back again. She wrote notes on a folded piece of paper, and measured the distance from where the car was parked to the driveway.

She stood by Spicey's car for a moment, watching everyone and everything, before joining them by the door.

"Come on hure, Mrs. Matty." Stank Stank called to her.

"Oh, we goin' in?" She asked, while scurrying over to the door, tugging at her blouse. "Ain been in no 'ho house b'fo. Ain takin' my clothes off either." She announced.

Punky stood behind her and held the door open. He frowned at the thought of a naked seventy something year -year-old woman, on stage, trying to strip and do a booty shake.

Gruesome looked at him and smirked.

"We go'n in da lounge area Mrs. Matty." Stank Stank told her. "We goin' to Spicey's office." "What you sey!" She said in surprise. "She gots husself a lil ole offis?"

She kept up with Stank Stank, anxiously awaiting to see the area Spicey considered an office. A few more steps and they made a left into another hallway and stopped. Stank Stank waved Gruesome up front to unlock the door and let everyone in. While they sat at a rectangular table, Spicey walked over to her desk and phoned Dope for some drinks.

"Would you like a drank momma Matty?" Gruesome asked the old lady.

"I guess I'll have a lil tonic wadda and gin, if ya got dat. Make sho it's in a small glass.

Anythang bigger and Mrs. Matty'll be up on dat stage shakin' ha tail betta than the 'ho who kilt Longskreet." She giggled. Gruesome gave her a smile, while Punky stood behind her frowning and shaking his head in disgust. She turned to Spicey.

"Now you know, ole Mrs. Matty just talkin'. I love you and Stank Stank there like you were my own." She told her apologethically.

Spicey ordered the drinks and made her way back to the meeting table. Gruesome alerted her to the major situation at hand. He told her how everyone got questioned except Sexie, who somehow made her way out of the bar and off the property, even though he'd called a lockdown. He told her how the area out back was taped off with police tape, while Punky supplied snapshots from his phone onto a vinyl movie screen.

"Puttin' ev'ra thang aside lil momma, you needin' a lawyer cause dey sey it's possible we could get shut down til dey can investigate thangs. Dat could take fo- fa six weeks." He told her in his low growl of a voice.

Mrs. Matty turned to Stank Stank. " What da Hell he talkin' 'bout? Caint nobody shut down ho'n. Jess cause da building gone, don't mean the queen done left the throne." She said and nodded.

"Yo, first thang I'd do is find Sexie." Punky advised. " Ween rat her out aw nuttin', but she had to have taken off for some reason."

Dope knocked twice on the door and entered carrying a large serving tray with drinks on it.

His layered blond hair was parted in the middle and had black tips. His black designer jeans were sagging well below his waist, exposing his black and white superhero boxers.   For a unique appearance, he tucked in the front of his tuxedo tee shirt while letting the back hang low. Mrs. Matty leaned over to Stank Stank.

"Dessa white boy, ain't it?" She asked. Questioning his appearance. "Dessa white boy?" Stank Stank smiled at her and held her hand affectionately.

"He work here, Mrs. Matty." Stank Stank told her. "He Spicey's bartender. We call him Dope."

Mrs. Matty removed her chew from her mouth and placed it in a piece of foil she'd pulled from her purse.

"You got a baff-room in dis offis?" She asked. Spicey pointed to a door near her desk. Dope placed the drinks on the table and returned to the lounge area. Mrs. Matty soon returned from the bathroom, dragging her purse beside her on the floor.

"Aw right. Where da Dope Boy put my drank." She asked..

Spicey, starting to come around, rolled her eyes at her and pushed the small glass closer to the old lady. Just then, Dope came through the door with a snack tray and placed it in the middle of the table.

"Oh, dis nice. Dis real nice. Fancy nuts and lil crackas and thangs. Ain talkin' 'bout you now Dope boy. I mean deez lil crackas on dis table." She assured him with eyes wide open.

"Mrs. Matty like all people. Even white folk." She told him. She nodded her head for reassurance before sipping her drink.

"Iown know what to tell you, Boss Lady." Gruesome growled to her. He threw back a shot of whiskey, refilled his glass and got a piece of cheese from the tray.

Spicey sighed heavily and assured them. "I got this." She returned to her desk and started thumbing through an old old-style rolodex. The group looked at her and waited for an explanation. Suddenly, she paused.

"Omma stawt my own investigation. I got a man." She looked at Gruesome. "J.T., you remember Sir Bob?" She asked.

"Aint that that ole stuffy shirt white dude that talk like he from anywhere but here?" Punky interrupted.

"Yea mane. Dude sho' weird now." Gruesome said smiling at Spicey. "Might getcha a boyfriend yet Mrs. Matty." Punky teased, winking at her.

Mrs Matty got up and stood behind her chair. She ran both her hand down her lumpy body. "He cain't handle all dis. Mrs. Matty be droppin' it like it hot up in here." She told him.

Punky looked at her with a facial mixture of disgust and humor. "He's Australian. Spicey told them. "He stay in Adelaide, Australia."

"OOHOOO, Ole snap! Stank Stank recalled. "He luv him some lil sussa too!"

Mrs. Matty nodded her head approvingly. "Another John?" She asked. "Cain't keep no good ho down".

"Gruesome, open the baw tonight. We got money to make. I need to get home and make a phone call." She said. She waved Stank Stank and Mrs. Matty out the room.

"Take me home be'fo you go driving Mrs. Matty." She requested, while turning and winking at the old lady. "I gots work to do."

My life ain't great but it's worth livin'

Two sticks of dynamite,

and I'm cold chillin'

"You look familiar",

I stood to greet.

"Just cover yo' ass,

and take a seat."

Oh, yeah, I could be disposable,

not worth a thing.

Shimmy, shimmy, shimmy,

hear dem bells ring.

Hear dem bells ring.

Hear dem bells ring.

The lights go out.

Nothing but a rag,

and I, take the clout.

CLARKSDALE LONGSTREET

Clarksdale Longstreet had a weakness for good booze and trashy women. He loved a good time at whatever cost. As long as Margaret Longstreet was miles away, he'd play hard and live it up, underground style on the down low, in anyone's car except his own. Every week, he'd drive outside the county line to visit popular highway bars and strip clubs. When news got out that one of his associates from the yacht club had opened a dance and watering hole about fifty miles down the highway, he couldn't resist patronizing the place. As a yacht club member, it would be the right thing to do. Besides that, it was just so close to his usual hangout that it would be downright wrong, not to indulge. He was a hard hard-working man. He felt that he deserved a little escape every now and then. It was said that his new help would do anything for a C-note, and Llookongstreet, being the Mayor of Myron County and a descendent of a self-made millionaire, had all the C-notes he needed, including a dozen or so tucked away inside his wallet for special weekend business trips.

In his eyes, there was nothing sweeter than a plump rump ebony dancer with artificial blond hair, crazy long nails and crooked, gapped teeth squirming seductively to the beat of some idiotic, foul- mouthed rap tune.

Even at his home in the neighborhood of Williams Grove, in Myron County, he had transformed his guest house into his ultimate man cave. Much to wife Margaret's dismay, he had several posters of half-dressed rap video dancers in bright colorful booty shorts all over the walls of every room. Even the hallway displayed posters of ebony models with waist- length oddly colored hair with bulging camel toes wearing two- piece dance suits. They all seemed to have some kind of weird piercing or tattoo somewhere on their body, and he gloated every time he looked at them. In the onc- lane bowling room, he had constructed a quiet box. It was a small square room with just enough room for a chair or   two, his desk and his prize CB radio equipment. This area was designed to block out sound.

Once inside, he felt that he could say or do anything in peace and quiet.

It was in this room that he enjoyed leisure time by talking to truckers and other CB listeners under the handle "Much Needy."

Clarksdale Longstreet started CB radio channel 69 and made it his own private music channel.

When he was on air, he'd continuously hold down the talk button and play about three of his favorite rap songs before actually talking. At the end of the third song, he'd announce in his coolish voice possible, "Much Needy. Channel 69. I'm open". This announcement alerted listeners that he was free and ready to chat. On June 17th, only minutes after announcing that he was open, his dream came true. As he sat there flipping through an issue of Hip Hop Rump Shakers, he heard a graspy female voice come over the radio. She sounded intoxicated, but that didn't phase him one bit. He'd thrown out a line and caught an ebony blowfish. With a little cash and some white wine, he was going to make this a feast fit for a king.

"If you gots the money, I sho-nuff gots the time." She called out. Clarksdale smiled and wet his lips. He had the money and he knew, for sure, that he was in the house.

MARGARET LONGSTREET

Margaret Longstreet sat on the bench, in front of the grand piano, staring at the ivory keys. With a glass of red wine in her right hand, she thought of every reason imaginable for not leaving her wealthy husband of thirty years. She sipped wine and focused on the swirls of circles on the ceiling. Her once smooth swan neck was beginning to show lines and wrinkles like the inside of a wood log. Her dark brunette hair now showed strains of grey. There were bags and dark circles under her eyes, that she covered daily, with make, up for public appearances.

The maid, Shiquanna, who was barely thirty years old, had given her a jar of her grandmother's homemade face cream that was said to get rid of dark circles and bags under the eyes. Margaret, for some reason, feared using it. Shiquanna's grandmother's cream sat ever so patiently on top of the piano, where it had been for several months.

Margaret was never too sure that Shiquanna would be a good employee, especially since the time that she returned home from brunch with the ladies and found Clarksdale and Shiquanna in the middle of the foyer squirming and popping to the latest raunchy womanizing rap music. What if the gardener had seen them? It would have been all over the neighborhood!

"Ms. Mawgret, Omma make 'em hip fa ya!" She recalled hearing Shiquanna squeal out

while tossing around waist- length orange hair. Her drawn on eyebrows arched wickedly with every facial expression. Clarksdale was smiling wildly, like he had never been happier in his life.

"You gotta put yo hand on my booty like dis , Mr. Clogg." She told him, while jotting out a hip. It was simply the most perverted thing Margaret had ever seen in all her years as the rich man's wife. She flashed the whites of her eyes at Clarksdale, disapproving of his actions.

When he ignored her, she walked through to her bedroom, popped a pill, and laid down to nap.

BIC HARDCASTLE

Bic Hardcastle was the owner and producer of Jess like Dat Productions. He was heavily into blue movies and was a frequent visitor to Spicey's Hangout. He was said to be of Italian and Puerto Rican descent, but his sparkling blue eyes often made that questionable. He was six feet, four inches tall with a tanned complexion and weighed a solid one hundred and ninety-five pounds. He had wavy black hair and a soft, subtle beard. He had a solid build, with naturally ripped abs and a very inviting lower cut,; the kind that formed a V from the waist down. He was very seductive. His strong New York Italian accent could talk open the tightest chastity belt.

At the Hangout, he could often be found sitting at the bar ordering drinks on tab and watching the girls dance, while scribbling in a black notebook. When he saw a girl, he'd like to film, he'd approach her with a fifty- dollar bill wrapped around a business card that read Call for free Consultation. If she accepted the money, he'd pull her close, and in his smooth, somewhat deep accented voice, he'd whisper, "Damn momma! You look so good; I wanna pay you for consultation." With his warm breath inches from her earlobe, he'd take the initiative of caressing it with the tip of his moist tongue. It's not what he said that made him popular with the girls, but the accent behind the words and the softness of his rigid tongue.

Bic was an entrepreneur. He knew that in his line of work, he needed pretty girls. Two months earlier, he had picked up and hired two big girls at the buffet restaurant across town. They were pretty and very curvy, but Bic didn't like putting all his hens in one coupe. Even though the girls agreed to star in a few of his movies, Bic liked having backups and when he saw Sexy in her pink wig, he nearly fell off the bar stool. He liked the way she bounced around and jiggled on stage. He knew instantly that she could make him millions.

Unfortunately, to Sexy, he was small potatoes compared to the older politician, from Myron County that she just had to see every weekend. Bic had spent hundreds of dollars trying to buy time with Sexy so he could talk business with her. It was obvious that she liked him.

He found that out, on the side of the building, late one night between shows. After about thirty minutes with her back against a hard stucco wall, she accepted a two hundred dollar tip and said they'd talk. Somehow, no matter what, Mr. Myron County always seemed to get in the way and Bic was growing tired of his interference. "Perhaps he could have a talk with this geezer and see if he'd like to be an extra in one of his movies." He often thought.

Bic was no fool. He knew no one was interested in seeing a saggy, naked, old man, so his plan was to keep him fully dressed behind a dummy camera while real cameras rolled on Sexy from all angles. In his mind, it was a good plan and it was worthy of highlighting in his black notebook. Next step was to contact the old dude and have a little talk with him. Emano, Emano.

EARLIER THAT WEEK AT THE HANGOUT:

CLARKSDALE LONGSTREET
And
MACKLEWAYNE KING

Macklewayne King, a verteran cross country truck driver, sat with Clarksdale Longstreet at the edge of the stage watching a large screen television that played continuous hip hop rap videos. It was supposed to allow a little relief for those truckers who wanted a shower, some grub and a little fun. For Macklewayne, it worked out just fine. He could walk in with his own forty forty-ounce bottle of beer or get an ice ice-cold frosty mug for the same price. Besides that, he was hoping to see the new help he'd heard so much about over the CB radio. She was said to be a real work of art who loved money and white powder. Macklewayne looked at Clarksdale with questioning eyes. Clarksdale picked up his warm fourty -ounce bottle of beer and took a good long gulp and let out an enviable burp.

"You can keep the fries, just give me that shake!" He yelled out to the stage dancer , while smiling and jerking to the sound of rhythmatic drum beats. Macklewayne could see the lust in his eyes and decided to offer his own two cents.

"Mane, gettha hell outta hure. You don't know what to do wit dat." He teased, while helping himself to a handful of pretzels.

"White mane cain't hounda no black woman." He told him. He rubbed his crotch. "Dis hure kang. He bragged.

Clarksdale smiled at him and turned his attention back to the stage. Macklewayne continued. "See dat big ass booty, rat dare?" He pointed at a girl on the dance floor.

"The one in da cona. Whatchu gone do wit sumptin' like dat?" Before he could answer his own hypothetical question, Juicey came running towards them, all wild eyed, wearing a bright red spaghetti strap top with no bra and brown skin tightskin-tight brown jeans.

"Ummm, mmm, sho look Juicey to me!" Macklewayne said, while holding up a twenty twenty-dollar bill. Clarksdale gazed at her and winked, as he pulled a wodd of twenties out of his pocket and held it in the air. Juicey's eyes lit up like shooting stars in the darkened room. She rushed over to Clarksdale and stroked his cheek.

"You wanna see my room, pop pop?" She asked Clarksdale, while stroking his salt and pepper beard.

"Oh, oh, okay." Macklewayne said. "I got fo 'mo baby. Andrew ain't by hisself." He assured her.

Juicey pulled Clarksdale by the arm and led him to one of the private rooms down the hall. Macklewayne sat there glassy glassy-eyed, with his nostrils flared in anger.

"Oh it's like dat, huh?" He said in jealousy. "You ain't all dat. Nappy head ass, ain't ja'mammy, cracka lovin' ho!" He said to her in anger. Clarksdale looked at him and tilted his long neck bottle and smiled. Macklewayne starred briefly in disgust.

"Mane, fuck you!" He said, while moving over to another section of the club. He spotted a waitress and waved her over.

"Hey baby, did you see dat ole white dude, who was sittin' ova thure wit me?" He asked. Who issie?"

The waitress seemed uninterested unitl until he held up a twenty twenty-dollar bill. She quickly took the money and responded.

"What about him?" She asked.

Macklewayne smiled. "Well, who issie?" He asked.

"That was Cloggsdale Longstreet. He comes here sometimes when he don't want to drive down to Hank's Honky Tonk." She told him.

"Yeah, but who issie?" Macklewayne asked. "He own dis junt ah sump'n'?" "He's the mayor of Myron County." She informed him.

"A male! Macklewayne responded in shock. "Okay, aw'ight. Thank you baby."

"So, Mr. Male like him a lil 5hockit on da side." He thought to himself, while finishing his large bottle of beer. In the deepsouth, where Macklewayne was from, stuff like that just didn't happen.

He felt betrayed by Juicey and was developing a feeling of animosity towards Clarksdale with every bottle of beer he ordered. He sat there contemplating revenge by flirting with the big big-chested blond who was taking food orders. Silently, he sat there hiding his blood shot eyes behind darkened sunglasses, while waiting for Clarksdale to return to the lounge area. Hours passed in, what seemed like a matter of minutes. It was dawn and the place was about to close. Two off duty police men approached Macklewayne to advise him of the time. He awakened almost instantly when one of them touched his shoulder. He'd gone through one forty- ounce bottle and nine longnecks. His mouth was dry and he had a terrible hangover.

While stumbling back to his rigg, he saw Clarksdale walking across the parking lot to his car. Macklewayne frowned and climbed into his sleeper for a few hours rest before heading on down the highway. He felt that his chance of happiness had been, once again, stolen by the man.

JUICEY

It was a rainy morning. The clouds were heavy over the city and the temperature was a bit cooler than usual. Along the lengthy stretch of highway, you could see the rainwater being pushed along by endless showers from above. There was a pungent smell in the air that went mostly undetected by passers-by on their way to connect with better jobs or bigger expressways. Along this lonely, deserted road were two well-known stops.

For patrons in need of special treatment from a seemingly respectable bar setting, about ten miles north was Spicey's Hideout. For those seeking beer, grubb, a side of pool and line dancing, there was Hank's Honky Tonk bar and grille. Due to the huge paved parking lot, this became a favorite stop for truckers looking for a few hours break before continuing on the open road.

Hank's Honky Tonk was a well maintained western bar with a large shiny wooden floor that was perfect for boot-scootin'. There was a bar area for those who wanted to sit alone and reflect on their thoughts, as well as a dining area with booths and tables. There were even socializing rooms, complete with sectional sofas and large flat screen televisions.

Hank's was a unique gathering spot. It stayed neat, clean and full of patrons.

Jezebel's Cleaning Crew had been hired to maintain the place. Jezebel's was given the contract because of Juicy Johnson.

One week night, when business was slow, Juicy arrived with a trucker from Texas.

While having drinks and truck-hopping, she mentioned how well the people she worked for could clean a hardwood floor.

Amazed that she had an actual job, the owner offered her a better paying gig. A chance to work at Hank's. When she said that she had no transportation to a place in the middle of nowhere, on a regular basis, he took her around back and offered her the attached studio apartment. Though only big enough for one person, it was just fine for Juicey. Two days later, she moved in and had a CB radio tower installed. Shortly afterwards, she was in business.

Juicey sat in the middle of the apartment, leaning over the glass table. Her baby doll nightie was stained with coffee from earlier in the morning. Her orange and black weave looked knotted and greasy but none of this mattered because she didn't have to start cleaning the bar until 3 o'clock. At this moment, all she wanted was what she had earlier. She tied her hair back and licked at the white dust that was still on the coffee table. Rubbing her hands along the edges and sucking at her lips, she looked around the room, wildly, for her hobo handbag. Spotting it across the room, she sucked her fingers and ran over to it, grunting eagerly, as she dropped her bare bottom onto the outdated carpeted floor.

"I know I got some mo." She said to herself. "Mama ain't gave all udd away."

She searched in her handbag for nearly five minutes and finally pulled out a tiny zippered plastic bag. She sighed with relief and ran back to loveseat in front of the coffee table.

Noticing the red stain on the small couch, she pushed the pillows and blanket aside and winced.

"Somebaddy must've spilt dey whyne." She said, while emptying the bag onto the glass top. She inhaled deeply through her nose and leaned back.

Her eyes were wide and glassy. The nighty barely hung onto her body as she sat there in a world only she could imagine.

Within minutes she began to jerk and giggle as she viewed old fashioned street- cars passing through the room.

A clientele of rich patrons waved hundred dollar bills at her and she tried happily to grab them out of the hands of each man.

"Slo yo' ass down!" She yelled out to no one. Suddenly, she saw a huge merry go round with Clydesdale horses. It took up all the space in front of her and even went up the wall. She stood up and walked over to the corner to climb onto the prettiest horse she saw.

Sadly, all she could do was lift her leg and touch the wall. She repositioned herself into a squatting position, holding onto the imaginary leather saddle of a horse, that never was. In her head, she could hear the circus music blasting in the evening air. Smelling the cotton candy, she licked her lips again, tasting sweet residue of the powdery substance.

She blinked her wide, dry eyes and started motioning as if she was throwing a ball. "Omma win the bure dis time." She said; barely able to stand still. She threw another Imaginary ball and began jumping up and down. She opened the door of the apartment and ran out into the parking lot, screaming and yelling in excitement while running around in circles. She awakened several sleeping truckers who gawked at her tripping, practically naked, outside in broad daylight. Realizing she had spectators, she lifted the sheer nighty and flashed her bare bottom to them as an invitation.

"I hit da red dot and won dat bure" "She yelled at o them."I bet you caint hit my ass in front of yo face!" She challenged. Prancing around barefoot in the dirt, she bowed gracefully and dashed back into the apartment, tore off the nightly and picked up the radio receiver. Eager to make more money to finance her addiction, she began to advertise.

"Breaker, breaker one-nine, you got da money, I sho gat da time." She laughed into the mike. "Any you boys wonna party with a happy gurl on a lonely highway. Over?"

For three seconds, there was nothing but static. Then, several responses tried to come through at once.

"Where you at pretty lady? What's your handle?" One trucker asked anxiously. "Route 87, bar and grille on left at 47 junction." She answered. "I be Jaye."

"Well, I be Damn! Miss Jaye. I'll be headin' ur way in about three hours if your free." The lonely trucker offered.

"If I aint, I will be." She said. "I'm out."

Looking out the window and only seeing three trucks, she felt the need to strum up more business for herself and for the bar and grille.

"Breaker, breaker two-fo, my good time is ova and om lookin' fo mo'. Come back." "Ooo Wee! Say it like you mean it than." One man came back with a growl in his voice.

"Where you be suggaplum?" He asked. "I got a partner. You up for a good ole fashion train ride tonight? We jest two purfect gents with two pocket fulls of dollas and cents."

Getting more and more excited by the minute, while calculating her prices, Juicey once again gave the location of the establishment. After hearing sirens nearing her area, she became paranoid and quickly turned off the CB. Grabbing an old dirty, fuzzy, blanket, she crawled to the green stained sofa and curled up on top of it. When the sirens were gone, she smiled peacefully; knowing her extra money and possible dinner was only a few hours away and she was safe.

EASYSLIDE

Easy Slide sat in the garage apartment behind his mother's house counting his weekly earnings. He'd bought a six six-pack of Raging Bronco beer, at the liquor store, where he'd cashed his check. He was almost done with the first can when he heard his mother's voice.

"Pooky, you gone eat suppa wit me biffo you run out in dem skreets?" The woman asked. At fourty -two years old, she was already missing several teeth and was constantly coloring her premature gray hair.

"Om commin' momma!" He yelled through the side door.

He put forty-five dollars and a glow-in-the dark condom inside a money clip and put it in his pocket. Realizing that he needed money for at least two drinks, he removed another ten dollars from his sock drawer and added it to his date money. He walked towards the door and turned around, quickly, returning to the drawer. He pulled a fifty fifty-dollar bill from the leftover bundle of ones and tens and put it in his shirt pocket. That was for his mama.

He had to give her some money. She was his heart. When he walked into the house, his mother was sitting on the couch watching some crazy sit-com from the nineties.

"Boy, brang yo' slo ass on in here so we can eat. Yo mama babyin' yo ass and goin' on like you still a school boy." A raggedy, graspy voice said from the other room. Easy Slide could hear his daddy's walking stick stabbing against the wooden floor as he made his way up the hall into the living room.

"You need yo' own home is what you need. Lazy ass rascal. Eatin' up my food. You a mane now. Get yo' own. Twenty Twenty-five yeels ole and aint got a pot ta piss in au a winda ta throw it out." Sisko scolded.

"Leave the boy alone Sisko. Heen done nothin'. " His mama pleaded.

"He sho ain't done nothing." Sisko replied. "Issa damn shame too."

"Why you always trippin' mane?" Easy Slide asked. His daddy looked at him and sighed deeply. "Boy, when I was your age, I had my own place. My own caw. A good job at the mill and was on my way to retirement, where I am now. Not yo' ass. You ain't got shit! Make me ashamed to tell folks you my boy." He lied.

"Maybe I ain't yo' boy." Easy Slide mumbled. "Witcho old ass."

Easy Slide looked on the dinner table and saw a stack of small oval sandwiches, homemade fries, and a bowl of pinto beans.

"Oooo Mama!" He yelled excitedly. "You made pig ear sliddas?"

"Yeah baby." She answered. "You can take some back in the garage witchu too."

He smiled widely, flashing his shiny yellow yellow-tinted teeth, as he leaned over and planted a kiss on his mama's cheek. He reached into his shirt pocket, pulled out the fifty dollar bill and gave it to her.

"Looka here!" Sisko yelled, pointing to the small color TV sitting on top of the wall shelf.

"Ain't dis dat place one yo frenz run au somethin? Dead white mane? Ole Hell. Somebaddy goin' ta jail if dey don't kil em first."

Easy Slide looked at his watch. "I gotta go call Stank Stank. I'll find out what happened tonight when I get there."

His mama was busy putting food on his plate and bagging up sliders for him.

"See Dat's yo problem rat dare. I see why you ain't never got no money. You get a lil money in yo pocket and (he claps his hands together and swiftly slides the other hand forward into the air) off to da hairy bank you go! Bookity-bookity-bookity!" Sisko fussed.

"Mane, I jess gave momma some money!" Easy Slide yelled, while wrinkling up his face in playful anger.

"Don't be gettin' huff wit me." Sisko told him, as he reached across the table to retrieve the single bill. He looked at it and gave it to Lolita.

"Diss don't pay no rent, big foolish, jugg-headed nigga! Where my damn case of beer you hauled outta here last weekend? Where dat at?"

Easy Slide shoved the second slider into his mouth and quickly slurped down the bowl of beans. While Sisko was busy watching the special news report, Easy Slide opened the frig and rushed down a can of pre-mixed rum and coke. He dashed past Sisko and let out a loud belch and yelled out to his mama.

"Love ya mama!"

"Bye baby. Love you too." She yelled back.

"If you need prophylactics; go buy some. I'own need no dumb, lazy ass gran-bel-studs runnin' roun here." Sisko told him in anger.

When his daddy looked up, EasySlide was tossing an empty can into the garbage. Sisko raised his walking cane and tried to hit Easy Slide across the back.

LOLO AND SISKO

After dinner, LoLo and Sisko returned to the living room to watch more of the local news. Seated on the couch, next to his wife, Sisko listened to the young children playing in the neighborhood streets. Suddenly, a feeling of nostalgia filled his heart as he thought about his own childhood. He lit a skinny, cherry cherry-flavored, cigar, leaned over and placed an arm around his wife.

Blowing a stream of smoke out of the corner of his mouth, he quietly sucked food particles from between his teeth.

"Lolo, you ever tell dat boy 'bout Lazelle?" He asked.

"Aint nothin' to tell him. She replied. "I nevva gotta chance to tell Lazelle I was pragnutt.

Heen won't no babies and I was the reason my baby was bone." She paused and giggled. "My grum momma used to sey, when you do wrong, wrong come to ya. She was sho right 'bout dat."

Sisko pulled her closely and kissed her on the cheek. His breath reeked of cherry tobacco. "All, you must've throde yo sweet, pruddy chum on him and he couldn't help hisself, huh?" Sisko wooed.

Not wanting to admit the actual truth, Lolita glared across the room at a picture of a two year -year-old Easy Slide and smiled.

"Dat's my baby dare." She told him.

"Come moan baby. You never did tell me how you ended up with him. You usta be at all dem stands, handin' out rubbas and pills and thangs. I was kind of sa'prised when you told me you was like dat." He admitted. "I was in love withcha tho. Pruddy 'lil ole thang you was.

Dats when I knowed I could getcha". He kissed her on the cheek and giggled like a school boy. We been murried now twitty fo yeels. Don't you thank you should tell big diddy? Ain goin' no whare baby. Om hure til Om cawled on to glow-ree."

Lolo held her head down in shame. "Lazelle had done came to owl house. Muldaire was at werk. I was at home by myself. We were kids Sisko." He squeezed her shoulder. "I know baby. I know." He soothed the tears swelling up within her eyes. We didn't know no better. We jess thought we were doin' what grown folks do when dey alone and feelin' like dat."

Sisko interrupted. "Well, we do. Don't we?" He asked. "Hehehe."

Lolo continued, too embarrassed to respond to his interruption. "I gave him a lil sump-sump tin." When we had finished, his beepa went off and he used owl phone. Then   all of a sudden he was grabbin his clothes and was on his head to get out da house. I   thought he musta been smelling behind Zelda. She was the only girl on owl skreet who had gone off to college and dent have no baby. Hur and Lazelle was around da same age and I hurd Muldaire and hur friend women talkin' 'bout what a good couple day would make.

Evry baddy was talkin' bout how much Lazelle like- did Zelda, but sheen have no time for a boy likc him. Hc wontcd his money right den, not no fo years later after he got outta no' school.

She had done came home for Sprang Break. I knowed dat, and when he jumped up, grabbing his clothes telling me, "I gotta go!" I grabbed his lil ole bill folda and ran to Muldaire's bedroom, got in her sewing bagsit, got the smallest needle I could find and put three tenny tiny holes in both dem rubbas he had." Sisko giggled. "You know dat was low down Lolo."

"Then I took his lil ole five dollas and threw it at him. He grabbed it up off the flo and shot out the dough like a bullet." Lolo told him. She looked back at the picture of the smiling toothless toddler.

"I paid fudd." She continued. "We made up the next weekend. We snuck into Gill-yen Pogg late one night with a blanket and a couple flashlights. He had a fawty of malt liquor.

We drank. Smoked a little "M.J." rhet under dat big old leaning Oak tree. Big ole pretty moon. Wind blowing softly and shit." She blushed a little.

"Six weeks later, I realized he must've used dem same two rubbas I put dem holes in, cos I was good and pragnut. By the time I got up the nerve to tell him, he got arrested and put in jail. I couldn't tell nobaddy fo sho afta dat. Den you came asking me out all the time. I had a baby on the way. You had a job and a podd ment and cah." She shrugged her shoulders and stopped talking. Sisko looked at her sympathetically and nodded.

"You toll me tho." He said. "You told me you was gone have a baby. Dat's why we still togetha. You ain toll no lie. Tha Hell wit Lazelle. Dat boy mine! I done fed him. Raised him. Beat his azz. Put clothes on his back. Hell! He still wearin' the draws I bought him." He laughed. "Lazy rascal." He kissed her cheek and smiled. "I sho' love him tho. Jess like I love you." He assured her.

SIR BOB OF ADELAIDE

Sir Bob sat intensely at his desk, going over notes and enjoying a fresh Tim Tam. Business had been slow this month and he had plenty of time to relax and hang out on Gougar Street with his friends and other investigators, engaging in thrill thrill-filled evenings of Mystery Theater, at the steakhouse. He took another bite of the Tim Tam and sipped absinthe from a cocktail glass. He leaned back in his swivel chair and stared at the ceiling while banging and slamming noises erupted from the kitchen. His housekeeper, Paige, was the daughter of an associate. Being a freshman in college, Sir Bob was sure she could use all the extra money she could get. Besides that, after briefly dating her mother, he felt obligated to help her out by letting her clean his apartment two days a week.

She was a quiet girl. Almost shy- like when speaking. However, her cleaning routine could wake the dead.

"All done Sir Bob." She announced timidly, while walking towards him and drying her hands on her well well-worn jeans. "If there's nothing else, Imma grab mi self a roadie and be on mi way."

Sir Bob blew smoke from his mouth, smiled and shooed her on. It wasn't a display of rudeness but a sign that he was in deep thought over a case he was working on. She understood and left quickly, letting the door slam behind her.

The telephone rang loudly, nearly startling him. He leaped forward in a rush to answer it.

"Sir Bob." He answered into the receiver. The old old-time phone cord was short and forced him to stay near his desk.

"Spicey!" He called out after recognizing her voice. "What a wonderful surprise. Are you ready to come Down Under for a week or two?" He asked with anticipation. Smiling happily, he leaned back, placing a bare foot upon the desk and entangling the phone cord between his toes.

"I need yo services dis time." Spicey told him. He could hear the seriousness in her voice.

"What's the trouble, love?" He asked, reaching for a memo pad. Spicey told him about the homicide behind the bar. He listened silently.

"Long story short, dey tryin' ta shut me down 'til dey finish investigating. I could lose a lot of money. Dey caint shut me down. I gots shows scheduled and paid for. Like most successful businesses, she told him, I don't do refunds. You feel me?" She asked. Spicey paused briefly, trying to hide the fact that she was worried to tears. "My girls might be cheap, but dey aint killas. I knows my people." She said.

Sir Bob scribbled "Homicide" on the top of the memo pad and poured himself another glass of absinthe.

"Has anyone been arrested or questioned?" He asked? "Are there any suspects in this case? What about witnesses?" He struggled to get a feel for the case.

"I've been out sick." She explained. "It happened yesterday." She lowered her voice to that of a well well-experienced seductress. "You know I'll take care of you, even if it means spending a few weeks at your place".."

The next morning Sir Bob boarded an airplane bound for the United States. How could he resist such temptation?

In the reclined seat, he listened to classical music through tiny earbuds and ate his fill of finger sandwiches. He slowly went over what little information Spicey had provided while waiting, patiently, for the plane to land.

Some twenty hours later, Sir Bob checked into his hotel room near the airport. His first order of businesses was to view the body of Clarksdale Longstreet.

THE MORGUE

Sir Bob went to the city morgue within hours of his arrival. The body of Clarksdale Longstreet laid on a metal table with a white sheet covering his midsection. Sir Bob put on a pair of latex gloves and began to inspect his hands and fingers. All of his fingers showed signs of a struggle. The purple bruising seemed to have been more intense on the fingertips of the left hand. This told Sir Bob that Longstreet was most likely left left-handed, and this hand possessed most of his strength. The fingertips showed mild bruising but no broken bones or damaged joints. Sir Bob pulled a square magnifying glass from the pocket of his overcoat and got a closer look at the fingernails. With a nearby pair of tweezers, he pulled a strand of colored fiber from the broken nail of Longstreet's middle finger. He looked at the thin line around the neck area. Longstreet was obviously strangled from behind, by surprise. Again, he used his magnifying glass and studied the bruised area. The weapon appeared to have been strands of strong string. Perhaps some kind of synthetic fiber. Twine maybe. He spent nearly thirty minutes looking at the neck. He was able to tell that in such a panic, Longstreet had dug his own fingernails into his neck while trying to save his life. It was embedded in his neck from digging and trying to tug at something. Sir Bob gently removed another piece of fiber from the wound and placed it a small test tube along with   the first piece of fiber he got from the fingernail. To him, it seemed to be the same kind of material, but what kind still seemed to be a mystery.

After leaving the morgue, he decided to make a quick trip to the police impound. He needed to see the car Longstreet was driving.

Once at the impound lot, Sir Bob took a golf cart to the location of the two two-toned unmarked police cruiser. The case number was clearly displayed in the window. The outside showed no signs of vandalism or forced entry. *So, was his assailant already inside the vehicle? Did he know this person?* Could it have been a date gone wrong? According to the toxicology report, there were no drugs in his system, not even a smigit of alcohol at this point. His own speculation made him consider a visit to the scene of the crime.

With daylight quickly slipping away, Sir Bob quickly found the impounded car and sprayed the inside with luminol. He then proceeded to look for evidence. Unfortunately, none presented itself. He slammed the door shut and walked around to the driver's side, where Longstreet was found. Again, there was nothing. Just when he was about to walk away, a slight breeze blew through the area and a long, colored strain of fiber caught his eye. It was stuck on the headrest. Sir Bob moved in for a closer look. As he opened the door to remove the strand, he saw another one behind the driver set. It was a long shot, but Sir Bob felt that these loose strands of fiber played a major part in the strangulation of Clarksdale Longstreet. He removed the strands, placed them in a small plastic bag and hurried back to his hotel room.

Since Longstreet was into CB radios, Sir Bob had a mobile unit set up in the bedroom. Within a few hours, a name came across the air that made him yell, "Eureka!"

It was a trucker named Macklewayne who spoke of hooking up with Longstreet for a few drinks and skirt skirt-chasing. Poor fellow sounded like he was unaware of what had happened.

Sir Bob pulled some strings and contacted Macklewayne King. Macklewayne made his way to the area just about every weekend. After informing the trucker of an important incident, Macklewayne agreed to meet with him for a brief discussion.

MCDENNEY'S TEA HOUSE AND COFFEE SHOPPE

Sir Bob waited patiently as the minutes ticked by. Macklewayne was forty-five minutes late and Sir Bob had gotten his fill of coffee and lattes. He scanned the room, hoping to pick the trucker out of the crowd that surrounded the front counter, but no one seemed to match the voice he'd heard over the phone.

Sir Bob had left word at the counter for the manager to point Macklewayne in his direction. Growing more and more tired with every minute, he checked his watch again. Fearing that the meeting wasn't going to happen, he removed a wifi tablet from his briefcase, and started typing in notes. His first entry read,"Meeting with Macklewayne King. 12:00 pm- Mcdenney's Tea House and Coffee Shoppe. He paused briefly to take in the soft sound of classical music, while inhaling the sweet smell of freshly baked blueberry scones. It almost reminded him of home. Instantly, out of nowhere, pulling him away from the peacefulness of the moment, was the loud roar of talk and laughter moving towards him. It was Macklewayne, all 6'4, 240lbs of him, in dusty, sagging blue jeans with dirty gloves hanging out the back pocket.

Across the front of his stained tee shirt, read the words, "On Time Trucking." He spoke loudly from across the room, as he made his way to the table.

"Hey mane! I know dat ain't no cap like da ones we wure 'round hure. Om willing to bet my last dolla, you dat dare dude from Gatalaide, aintcha?" He asked loudly.

Sir Bob took a small flask from inside his vest pocket and took a healthy swig of absinthe.

He tried unsuccessfully to shield it from Macklewayne, who swiftly approached him smelling of fresh cut lumber, corn chips, and raw onions. The boisterous trucker continued his loud greeting.

"Ahh, I see ya thure. I see ya gotcha a 'lil sumptn' sumptn'. Handle yo bitness poddna, ain mad at cha."

He grabbed a chair, turned it around backwards and sat down, manspreading, showing off the silver dollar sized hole in the crotch of his dusty stained jeans.

"Mane, Iown know what was happenin' today. Dat place I stay at, when om in town, ain't but ten minutes up da road. I swell traffic wuz a mulfucka." He said.

He looked at Sir Bob studiously, awaiting further explanation of the visit.

"Mr. King." Sir Bob said. "We're meeting today because I need to know how well you Knew Clarksdale Longstreet." He glanced up at Macklewayne to see if he heard the magic word. As you know, he was murdered a few days ago." He stated.

Macklewayne jerked his head backwards and bounced up and down, as his eyes flew open as wide as saucers.

"You gotta be shittin' me!" He said in surprise. "Who da hell? Mane, what da fuck? He done got kilt? He dead? Mane! Ain me. Ain seem him in two weeks." He said.

"I'm in town working on his case. How well did you know Mr. Longstreet?" Sir Bob asked. Macklewayne, still in shock, answered quietly. "Not to well. I mean, he'd come in the bah, have a drank or two with me. We'd chase some tail." He smirked a little and hesitated. "Cloggsdale always had 'mo money than I did, so he'd steal the bitch I had picked out fa da night and shit. Ween have no beef, though. I mean, Hell, caint get one 'ho, a nuttin' 'round da cona. I mean, I coulda beat his ass fudd , now, cause back in high school, I took dat dare karotty. I can kick a niggas ass if I wonts to." He said with widened eyes. Pimp slap 'em and all dat shit. Heheheh." He grabbed his crotch with one hand as if he was trying to close up the hole.

"How often are you in town?" Sir Bob asked again, while diagnosing every word of Macklewayne's answer.

"Om hure, every weekend or so. Sometimes I would run into him over at Spicey's Hangout.

Ain go there much dough. Dey got dis big niggah, who thank he's the beez kneez and the clam dip too. Heen nothing 'mo than a watchman fa da lady who own da junt. Shee-it, she was a big time 'ho husself, befo she opened the bah. Probably still one. You know what dey sey mane. Once a 'ho, always a 'ho." He said smiling and widening his red red-tinted eyes.

Sir Bob listened closely and jotted down what seemed important. He kept from interrupting Macklewayne, because he felt he could use this time to remember a lost friend. So, Sir Bob let him continue.

"My mane like-did them honeys tho.

He like-did them lil ole bubble booty dancers. The ones who could wrap dey legs up high on da pole and bounce it low on the flo. Somebaddy must've told him he was a brotha."

He looked up at a hostess. "Baby, can you brang me one of dem shokit moka lot-tays?" He winked at her.

"Add it to my tab." Sir Bob told her.

"All Hell!" Macklewayne said. "You tabbin' up in hure? Come moan maine, hook a brudda up wit a sammich den." Sir

Bob loudly cleared his throat and snapped his fingers in the air. The hostess, now two tables over, looked his way.

"May I please add a house club to that order, my dear lady?" He asked. "Certainly Sir." The hostess replied.

Macklewayne glared at him, smiling admirably. "See dat's how bitches respond to me at the clubs." He lied. "Dat kinda respect and shit."

"What kind of man was Mr. Longstreet?" Sir Bob questioned.

"Cloggsdale wonted to be a playa, but the only thang he had goin' for him wassa pocket full of money."

Macklewayne told him. "Hell, you flash fiddy dollas au so in a 'ho's face, she all ova it like stank on shit." Sir Bob sat patiently, waiting to hear something important. Macklewayne continued.

"He loved women of color." He said, winking at Sir Bob. "Dey sey, the dawker da berry, the sweeta da juice." He said, while smiling widely, just Just then, his food arrived. Sir Bob nodded slowly and returned one semi- confused wink.

"He loved hip hop, rap music, and big azz dawk gurls." Macklewayne told him. He took the top bun off his sandwich and flooded it with hot sauce and extra mayo before taking a huge bite. With his mouth still full of partially chewed food, he sipped the latte and continued. "My boy's cousin, he paused and swollowed some food, La La, usta work for him and his wife out at dey house. She a 'lil ole shawt thang. He held his hand up and apart, while making a half circle with them.

Big ole bubba booty and fat titties. Prutty 'lil thang, 'bout twinny fo yeels old, I guess. Cloggsdale was crazy 'bout her. Gave her tips wit ha paycheck and shit. Let her barrow expensive caws and thangs.

His wife put an end to all dat, called her in one day when Cloggsdale was at work, gave her two months pay and sunt her home. She was helping him download videos and thangs in his lil private room where he usta run some fake ass radio broadcast thang. You know, one of them Am stations only a few people listen to. His wife, sheen like all dat. Den La La went and bought him a copy of" Bouncin' Black Booty" Magazine and had it autographed by some porn star. She gave dat to him for his birthday.

Dat's who you need to talk to, La La. She might can tell you some thangs."

Sir Bob remained silent. He was making facial expressions and gestures as he entered information into a small handheld computer.

Macklewayne continued to eat his lunch, wiping his hands on his dirty jeans with almost every bite taken. When not smacking starvingly, on a bite of food, he slurped his latte loudly while looking around smiling at the hostesses. Once he finished eating, he turned   his head to the side and let out a loud uncovered belch that back-drafted into the face of Sir Bob, who immediately placed a napkin over his nose and continued to scan collected notes.

When he was satisfied that Macklewayne was nothing more than a deep southern truck driver, he thanked him for his time and gave him a truck stop gift card.

"So I can go? We done?" Macklewayne asked, while quickly taking the gift card from his hand.

"Yes, Sir Bob responded, as he stood from the table, good day sir."

"Hang on maine." Macklewayne said to him, as he dug out a large raggity overstuffed chained wallet from his back pocket. "Here a bitness codd I got from dis chick who usta do thangs for Cloggsdale every now and then. Maybe she can help you".

Sir Bob read the card aloud in disbelief. "Mi'sexie A. Butt?"

Macklewayne gigled and rubbed crumbs from his mouth. "She seh it's pronounced, My Sexie. I caint say nothin' tho.

Hell, if I had a little baby girl that I knew was gonna grow up to be sexy like she is, I'd name her something bold and proud too. Folks cain't help dey last names. Hurs jest happen to be Butt." He said. Macklewayne saluted Sir Bob and walked out.

BELLE TOWER HOTEL

ir Bob filled the bathtub with multicolored bubbles and soothing hot water. He added a splash of lavender lavender-scented baby oil and stripped to his blue and gray gun printed boxers. He wrapped the thick, cotton bath towel around his partially nude body and called for room service. He needed more absinthe. It would be late evening soon and he wanted to relax and go over notes before bed. He'd been to the morgue, he'd spoken with the truck driver and still something just was'nt setting right in his mind. He needed more. He walked over to his desk, sat down and removed a cigar from the drawer.

As he leaned back in the chair, drawing in the flavor of the fresh cigar, he heard a faint knock on the door.

"Please enter!" He called out, from across the room.

The door opened slowly, causing suspicion. Sir Bob reached for his dillinger and waited. A mixture of mint mint-scented muscle rub and flowered perfume began to fill the air.

"Please come in," Sir Bob repeated.

The visiting stranger appeared to be a mature woman in her mid to late sixties. The kind he enjoyed spending time with from time to time. Her eyes were covered with big dark sunglasses, and a knit scarf covered her head. She wore a long black trench coat, ankle socks, and beige orthopedic shoes.

"May I help you." Sir Bob asked politely. " Are you lost, my dear?"

"Hell nawl, ain lost." The woman responded. "I knows who you is and dats why om here. Now hold on a minute, let me close dis dough. Folks don't need to know my bitness." She pushed the door closed and removed the scarf. Walking a little closer, she took off the sunglasses and gave him the most serious expression she could.

"My name Clara Matty." She told him. "You workin' on a case for Spicey Robinson."

Sir Bob stood up and eyed the old woman from head to toe, as tons of questions raced through his mind. *What secrets could she possibly tell him? What does she know? Could she, herself, be the killer?*

Perhaps, she would stay for dinner, as they discuss things.

Sir Bob removed the cigar from his mouth and placed his hand in the pocket of the robe, gripping his Dillinger, just in case. For experience alone, had taught him to put safety above everything, especially, loneliness and lust.

"So, you know Mrs. Robinson?" Sir Bob asked inquiringly.

"Know her?" Mrs. Matty responded. "You mydis websta say I buffed her."

"I beg your pardon?" Sir Bob said. "I don't understand." Remembering Spicey as a newborn, Mrs. Matty gave an adoring smile. "Been knowing her since she came out her momma's womb. Lil bitty thang, she was. Came 'bout six weeks ully. Her brother, he was lookin' forward to a lil sister too.

He was just jumpin' 'round all happy and stumblin' ova thangs. He was just stawtin" to walk good hisself. Anyway, that's why om here. Spicey a 'ho. She mi-yeer the biggest 'ho around, but she my girl.

I'd do anything I can far her and her brudda. Them two like my own." She told him, while removing the trench coat.

Realizing that she was nothing more than a gentle, caring individual, Sir Bob spoke up, "Oh, please, by all means, make yourself comfortable." He told her, taking the coat and laying it aside.

"Legal folk tawkin' 'bout shuttin' her down, making her lose money while dey investigates. Could take months. All dis cos some hot in the britches male got hisself kilt."

"Have a seat, Mrs.?" Sir Bob hesitated, trying to remember her name.

"Matty!" She told him. "Everybody knows Mrs. Matty. You know dirt on the ground; you know Mrs. Matty." She smiled. "Now I'own mean no hum, so you can gone relax and put dat lil pistol back in da draw somewhere. Ain got no weapon, just a bag of evidence to show you."

Sir Bob smirked and put the Dillinger back in the drawer.

"How did you know where to find me?" He asked her.

"Mane, dis tha fanciest hotel in the city and you a Dee-tective. Dats how I knode you'd be stayin' here.

Spicey said, she was gone call you. I may be olda, but ain senile yet." She smiled. " Mrs. Matty got plenty sense." She said, while noticing the thick bush of graying hair peeking out from his partially covered chest. "Sho do smell pretty in here." She told him.

"I was about to take a soak." He told her. His eyes met her gaze. Just then, there was a knock at the door.

"Room Service!" The young man yelled from the hallway.

"I'd better get that." Sir Bob said, rising from the chair. His bathrobe falls loose, slightly exposing his thin, gun printed boxers. Mrs. Matty smiled approvingly and nodded at his statement.

"Coming!" He yelled out, while pausing briefly to grab a few dollars from a brass tray. "Your fifth of Absinthe Sir." The young man said, while wheeling in a cart. He placed the crystal bottle and two shot glasses on the small coffee table in front of the love seat and retrieved two seven inch candles from his pocket and lit them. He looked at the two of them and smiled. Sir Bob reached in his robe pocket and pulled out a thin stack of one one-dollar bills. He counted out five and gave them to the attendant, who nodded appreciatively and left the room.

"Please join me here on the sofa and show me your evidence." Sir Bob said to Mrs. Mattie. He extended an arm. She quickly obliged. He poured two shots of Absinthe, sat down on the sofa and handed one to Mrs. Matty. She sipped it immediately.

"This is my poison of choice." He told her as he guzzled down the liquid. "It is tasty." She replied, smacking her mouth before downing the liquor.

Sir Bob cleared his throat, as the alcohol raced to his head, giving him that relaxing feeling he often craved after a long day's work.

He then crossed one leg and leaned closer to Mrs. Matty. "Now, about this evidence?" he asked quietly.

His voice dropped an octave. "What do you have, and by all means, how did you get it?" He leaned forward and filled their glasses again.

Mrs. Matty sneaked a quick admirable look at his wavy salt and pepper hair, noticing his fashionable haircut. It was after seven in the evening and Sir Bob's five o'clock shadow was in full bloom. Atop his smooth olive skin was a thick dark patch of stubble that matched the coarse hair that peeped out from his chest.

"To solving the case." He toasted. He handed the other glass to Mrs. Matty, who in return, tilted her glass towards his.

"You know, I don't usually drank dis much liquor without food. It can make you crazy. Even I know dat." She told him, just before inhaling the alcohol in one gulp.

"Well, Mrs. Matty, it is that time. Won't you join me in a dinner for two?" He asked.

The sun was setting and the interior of the penthouse was darkening. The candles began to cast a soft glow upon the walls, as a certain kind of warmth began to fill the room. In the candle light, Mrs. Matty focused on the flames glowing in Sir Bob's pale blue eyes. Pulling herself away from his hypnotic appeal, she suddenly turned her head and cleared her throat.

"I see you're the kind of woman who enjoys fine liquor as much as I." He said.

"Now, about dinner? My treat." Mrs. Matty put her knees tightly together and adjusted her cleavage.

"Well, om here and you here." She smiled. "What we havin'?"

Sir Bob thought briefly and announced, "Lobster Cantonese, with fried rice and vegetables. A favorite of mine." He brushed a strand of hair from her face. "I'd love to feed you your first bite." He flirted.

He stood up and walked over to the phone. "I'll order room service and place our order.

You should refill our glasses." He suggested. The room was now dark, but glowing. Sir Bob made his way to the desk. He lit a cigar and placed a call to the kitchen. Feeling the effect of the alcohol, he glanced questionably at Mrs. Matty, as he tried to make heads or tails out of his intentions. He had to have been at least seven years her junior, just the way he liked it, but was she willing?

"mmm,mmm, I've always like did the smell of a good ciggaw." Mrs. Matty said. "Dat smell so good to me."

"It couldn't possibly smell as good as your perfume, my dear." Sir Bob wooed. He went and removed a box of Tim Tams from his drawer of goodies and made his way back to the love seat, stopping briefly to adjust the volume of the, in wall, mp3 player. It seemed to have been programmed to play a variety of old 1970 style sex music.

"Would you like a snack before dinner?" He asked her, placing the treats on the table. "These are as sweet and chocolaty, as you are." He smiled. "It's a common snack back in Australia." Mrs. Matty was beginning to feel like she was back in college again. In her right mind, she knew what was happening, but her right mind was lost in a warm, steamy fog of growing passion, complete with a free lobster dinner and the company of a younger gentleman from another country. Something she had never experienced before. The soft music alone was enough to melt away any doubts. Yet, they were both adults. Intoxicated, consenting adults. Mrs. Matty, in an attempt to stop or slow down what was happening, grabbed her purse and withdrew a plastic sandwich bag. She handed it to him, just as he hand fed her a piece of the chocolate biscuit.

"You're some kind of woman, Clara Matty." He told her. He looked briefly at the bag. He saw nothing more than bits of trash, but the fact that she would go to such an extent to help someone made her more appealing than ever to him. She was simply a woman with love in her heart for everyone. He moved closer, sneakingly placing his arm around her, as he looked at the contents of the bag again.

"Clara, I'm afraid you're going to have to explain all of this to me. I'm not as focused as I should be." He admitted. "Please pardon me if I'm too forward, but in this light, your beauty is exhilarating."

It was a little after nine, the next morning. Sir Bob awakened to find that he was all alone in the pillow pillow-topped king size bed. He could smell a pot of fresh coffee brewing. It was slowly covering up the aroma of last night's lobster dinner. He called out for Mrs. Matty, even though he knew there would be no response. In his eyes, Clara Matty wasn't the type to hang around after what she thought to be a one night stand.

She'd ordered breakfast and left it for him. Sir Bob got up, grabbed his robe and made his way to the desk to plan his day. He sat down to check his notes. Almost instantly, he got a swift of Mrs. Matty's flower scented perfume. He smiled at the reminder of what was and reached for a morning cigar.

Next to the phone was a note from Mrs. Matty. He poured a cup of coffee, lit the cigar and prepared to read what he thought would be nothing more than a peaceful good-bye.

To his surprise, the mature woman that he'd spent the night with, had left him with leads. Somehow, she really did have something other than bits and pieces of trash in a sandwich bag. She gave names, locations and people to talk to. He grabbed a map and a magnifying glass. He scanned it thoroughly, looking for a place called Crystal Town. She said that it was on the far outskirts of town near the city dump. It was a small neighborhood full of thugs, crackheads, ex-cons and rooming houses. There were supposed to be two or three streets with nothing but shotgun houses side by side. There, I was to find and question one of her old classmates.

Rumor had it that some years ago, someone made a threat to this Longstreet fellow after a court hearing, but nothing ever came of it. Now, two to three decades later, Longstreet is murdered.

He was to find the whereabouts of Patrick Funk, Jr. kKnown on the street as P. Funk. Sir Bob reached over and grabbed the burning cigar. He couldn't make heads or tails out of P. Funk, but his gut told him not to dismiss it just yet. He scribbled Crystal Town and P. Funk, jr. on a piece of paper and got dressed. He glanced over his original notes and saw where someone had mentioned the disappearance of a dancer, by the name of Sexy. It would be interesting to find out why she disappeared when the police arrived at the scene. Time was ticking, and if possible, he needed to get by the scene of the crime before continuing on to Crystal Town. He got dressed and headed out. In the back of his mind, he wanted to find Mrs. Matty and properly thank her, but she 'd left no contact information.

THE SENIOR CENTER

Back at the senior center, Mrs. Matty was walking around sipping diet soda and tasting finger sandwiches. She was supposed to meet Lillie there but, so far, there were no signs of her or her scooter.

Mrs. Matty pulled a hard plastic phone from the top pocket of her large handbag. After walking away from the crowd, she found a padded bench in the hall and sat down.

"Whatchu doin' there old lady?" A voice called out. Mrs. Matty, biting on her bottom lip while trying to focus on the numbers on the phone, never looked up.

"Iown know who you callin' old lady, but it sho ain't me". ." She responded, thinking it was just another senior interrupting her.

"Matty hang dat damn phone up. You know it's me." Lillie said. She zoomed her scooter up next to Mrs. Matty. Mrs. Matty finally looked around and saw her.

"Who you callin' old lady?" She repeated. "Old ladies caint do the thangs I can do." She told Lillie.

"Whatchu mean Mattie?" Lillie asked her. "Chew on dat snuff and get in folks bitness?" She laughed teasingly and hugged Mrs. Matty.

"Tell me, you been tryin' to shake yo tail at Spicey's 'ho house." Mrs. Matty told her. "I mighta been tail shakin', but it wudn't at no ho house". ." Lillie told her.

She looked momentarily at Mrs. Mattie in a questionable way, but said nothing.

Mrs. Matty was proud of the fact that she had a secret that may help save Spicey's bar.

Unfortunately, she had mixed feelings about how things went down. She saw the way Lillie had looked at her, but pretended she didn't. She pretended to be busy placing the phone back in her bag.

"Look at dat there Matty." Lilly said while pointing at an old slickster, barely walking, making his way toward them.

"Mmm,mmm." Mrs. Matty said, shaking her head. "Thad eels." "There what is Matty?" Lilly asked.

"A cryin' shame." Mrs. Matty told her.

Lilly slapped her leg and laughed as the older gentleman made his way towards them.

Mr. Slugg was nearly eighty years old and lived up to his name. He moved his feet about   an inch at a time. He was often seen chasing any lady within his sight, as fast as his feet and walking stick would allow. Every woman was at risk when the old man Slugg was around. He adored them. Young, old, ancient, it didn't matter, as long as he could get next to them.

Mr. Bernardo Sluggensky wanted to be a smooth operator. His grandson told him that he had to be cool and sauve to get women to spend time with him. Sluggenky had been a widower for seven years and I guess an itch, of some sort, was finally developing and he wanted a good old fashioned scratch.

That's what ole Mr. Slugg was looking for. His current victims were Mrs. Matty and her best friend Lilly. He made his way towards them, looking as hip as he could in his black leather biker pants, and white tee-shirt. Around his neck, he wore a black studded choker that dangled a small gold bone from a half half-inch link chain. His matching black leather bracelet had a watch in the center of a cluster of rounded-tip spikes.

"Slugg, what da Hell iz all dat mess?" Mrs. Matty asked. "I know 'yo old tail ain't got no motorbike."

He smiled seductively, leaned over and placed an arm around her shoulder. They could

smell the expensive cologne he'd obviously poured over his body before leaving his house. "Hi, you ladies doin' tonight?" He whispered in her ear.

"We fine." Mrs. Matty responded. "You ain't gotta be all up on me." Mr. Slugg backed away from Mrs. Matty and stood behind Lillie. He started massaging her shoulders.

"I bet I can give you a massage, so good, you'll forget 'bout dis scooter." He told her. Lille, who hadn't seen any action or attention from a man in over a decade, giggled and blushed like a young school girl.

"You ladies ought ta come with me back home and let me sing to you. You know I sing." He reminded them. He started humming softly to them.

"Why you got a damn bone hanging from dat thang 'round yo nake?" Mrs. Matty asked suddenly.

Slugg put his hands on his hip and began to growl softly.

"Imma dog baby. This what you call doggy style." He said, winking at her. "I come here for some sweet treats."

"Try dem lot lilzuts at the truck stop cross the freeway. Tell me dey out all times of night giving out treats and thangs." Mrs. Matty told him. "Need to get his old red ass somewhere and sit down." She mumbled to Lillie, who checked her purse and released her parking brake.

Lillie giggled at Mrs. Matty's comment and smiled at Slug, who licked his lips and winked at her again.

"Dey 'bout ta stawd the game ya'll. We betta get on in da room if you wonna get some good codds." Lillie advised.

"We plan Euchre da night, ain't we?" Lillie asked.

The trio made their way into the game room and found a table. Everywhere they looked, there were photos of older mature people playing games and enjoying life just as they did when they were younger. On the wall behind them was a giant framed poster of an elderly couple planting a flag on top of Mount Everest. Below it, was advertisements for the newest medications for arthritis and joint pain relief. The entire room smelled of fresh popcorn, coffee and sweets. There was a small area in the corner where staff members sold beer, wine, soda and mixed drinks. On certain nights, such as tonight, they'd go as far as hiring a pianist to entertain the crowd. At least four other staff members, two nurses and a couple security guards entertained themselves from a small gathering room where they looked out and monitored the crowd. In the tv room, on the other side, those who were not into card games, gathered together to watch reruns of ancient detective shows on the big screen, that reminded them of younger days. They would sit there staring at the large flat screen tvs   like they were watching the number one "Who done it" movie of all time. Slugg started singing softly along with the pianist as he played a popular love song of the 1940s.

One of the staff members heard his trained voice and got the pianist's attention. She and Slugg made their way to another piano that had a microphone stationed on top.

The pianist started the song from the beginning and Slugg sang along, trying his best to please every woman in his presence. Even Mrs. Matty clapped and applauded for him.

"Gone den Notto Slugg!" She yelled out when he hit a deep note without cracking it. "Don't dat just send chills through yo spine?" Lilly asked while smiling at Slugg appreciatively.

When he'd finished, he whispered something to the musician and sang one more song dedicated to Lilly, before returning to the table. Ms. Lilly took a sip of her coffee and blushed as he sat down next to her. Within minutes, she felt a hand upon her knee, as Slugg leaned over and planted a kiss upon her cheek.

"Oh, Hell, nawl!" Ms. Matty told them. "Don't y'all be stawdin' no freaky-deaky mess up in here. We s'pose ta be plain codds. We need one 'mo playa. Anybody?" She called out as new members walked in. The seniors played four rounds of cards while Lilly and Slug giggled and made eyes at each other. After two hours and two glasses of gin and tonic, Mrs. Matty co co-started reminiscing about her own adventures with Sir Bob. At that point, she politely excused herself and went home.

CRYSTAL TOWN

Sir Bob arrived at the run-down halfway house near the city dump. It was a fairly large building with three sections desperately in need of repair. In the middle of the first section was an orange door with black graffiti spray painted all around the frame. Yellow police   tape blocked the entryway and specks of blood could still be seen on the pavement leading   to the narrow sidewalk. The atmosphere was gloomy and the stench of freshly cooked meth filled the air. One unit had two doors boarded up with wood. The door on the left had a broken out window next to it. Crushed malt liquor cans and cigarette butts topped the ground below.

Walking past the window welcomed you home with the pungent smell of old cigarette smoke and stale urine, breathing out upon you from within the darkness of the dilapidated dwelling. Sir Bob covered his nose with a folded handkerchief as he made his way past the horror before him.

The next section of the building was completely in use. In the distance, he could see tenants sitting and standing on concrete steps, consuming beverages from containers hidden by brown paper bags. Others stood around cursing, laughing and grabbing their crotches every few minutes. There was a parking lot across the street. A small group of men loitered around an old 1960s sports coupe. Their jeans sat so low beneath their waist that it made their legs look like they were two feet long. Sir Bob checked the side pocket of his plaid leather vest for his concealed derringer and took a sip of absinthe. He began to smell the aroma of a failed attempt to cover up reefer mixed with cigar tobacco. Yet, his investigation called for him to be where he was, so he sighed deeply and walked swiftly towards the entrance in search of someone by the name of Momma Lou.

Momma Lou was the owner and proprietor of Lulu's Half Steps. It was a low cost halfway house for nonviolent, ex-cons. All the talking and cursing stopped the moment Sir Bob was spotted by the group. He was glared at like rotten meat on a display counter.

One tall ragged looking man, with long grey and black dreads and no shirt, picked up a wooden baseball bat and patted his open palm with it while gazing steadily at Sir Bob with red drug drug-induced eyes. Sir Bob returned his stare and patted his right vest pocket, alerting the vagrant to what could be inside. The tall man smiled crookedly, flared his nostrils a few times and placed the bat against the wall.

"Good day gentlemen." Sir Bob greeted as he approached them. Two of the men gave him a blank face head nod, while others just looked and said nothing at all. The man with the dreads stepped forward. He smelled like a mixture of body fluids, smoke and dirt. His ragged splotches of a beard were knotted up in grey and black hair balls. Sir Bob managed to keep a straight face, while readying himself for confrontation.

"Can I help you wit sump tin?" He asked Sir Bob. His two front teeth were covered with a brown film that hid the yellowish tint that was visible on one side tooth. The way he tilted his head while questioning, revealed several missing teeth and a bad case of gingivitis.

Sir Bob smiled friendly and responded, "It would be quite lovely if you'd direct me to Momma Lou."

The other men repeated the words "quite lovely", while laughing and cursing among themselves.

"Skrate inside." The dreaded guy directed while pointing up to the double wooden doors.

Sir Bob entered the foyer very cautiously. He could see a huge heavy woman at a desk behind a long black piece of carpeting. Obviously, a receptionist of some sort. Sir Bob could hear typing from a distance. Immediately to the left was a set of stairs with a sign above that read "Rooms 2-14". As he slowly moved forward, a loud buzzer sounded and the women immediately spun around in the chair. Still looking at a piece of paper she was holding, she called out to him.

"Follow the strip of carpeting and place it on my desk or get the Hell out of my house!" She demanded sternly before glancing up at him.

"Oh, pardon me, ma'daam!" Sir Bob said every so politely. "I'm looking for a lovely young dame that goes by the name of Momma Lou." He said, as he made his way down the strip of carpeting and extended a hand.

"Well now." Momma Lou said, raising to shake his hand. Before she could say another word, Sir Bob took her hand, turned it over and planted a kiss on top, just above the knuckles. He sighed at the pungent smell of ginger and powdered perfume. Momma Lou smiled timidly and made her way around the front of the desk to greet him properly. She was a large bowling ball of a woman and by the time she made her way around the front of the desk, Sir Bob had produced a concealed weapons permit and handed it to her.

"I'm a reporter." He lied. "I've been asked to do a story here in Crystal Town. An associate of mine suggested that I feature your establishment since your tenants seem to have such a wonderful success rate when they leave here."

She smiled flirtingly at him and flickered her long fake eyelashes. "My boys come in here right from the joint, clean their acts up and start their lives over. If they aint serious, I don't take 'em."

She told him, while admiring his plaid vest. She went behind the desk and removed a large bottle of whisky and two shot glasses from a locked drawer. She handed one glass to Sir Bob, glanced at his gun permit and returned it to him.

She poured him a shot of whisky, filling the glass to the rim before filling her own glass and throwing it back in one shot. Sir Bob did the same.

"These rascals 'round here ain't doin' much. Just looking for easy work, collecting unemployment money and dranking it up." She admitted.

Sir Bob looked at the tacky Mexican decor that covered the wall behind her. Although it was clear that she wasn't of full Mexican descent, she seemed to favor colorful sombreros and photos of different el toreros. In the middle of all the wall clutter was a framed business license with the name Louisa Johnson. She filled her glass with tequila and handed the bottle to Sir Bob. He nodded gratefully and poured himself a drink. She stood beside him, smiling, as he looked at the mural of Mexico behind the clutter.

"My daddy was a bullfighter." She told him, while lighting a skinny cigarette. "There he is, over there, by the maracas." She pointed to the far corner. Sir Bob slammed the tequila down his throat and put the glass on a nearby table.

"Would you like a smoke?" Momma Lou asked. "This aint exactly a nonsmoking place." She said.

"I carry my own, thank you." Sir Bob replied while removing a cigar from his pocket. "You're awfully quiet for a reporter. Almost make me think you're undercover or something." She said.

"Actually, I am." Sir Bob told her. "Usually, when people hear I'm working on something for a magazine, suddenly everyone has a story." He walked over to the table and sat down. Momma Lou followed.

"So, is there anything I can help you with?" She asked. Sir Bob was a bit uncomfortable asking about her tenants right off the bat, so he pulled out his memo pad and asked about the halfway house. Eventually, he asked about her heritage. The surname Johnson, didn't strike him as being of Mexican descent. Yet, she had thick dark hair and smooth olive skin. She was surely Hispanic.

"My daddy was in the local Mexican -American War." She told him. "It wasn't real." "She told him. It was a neighborhood thing." She smiled. Sir Bob took it as some kind of inside joke and smiled back without question, so she continued. "He was a prize bullfighter in Mexico."

Mi Tio was shocked when they called him to war. He went peacefully, but returned to bullfighting when the war was over. That's when he met mi madre. She was a singer trying to get signed with a huge record company in Detroit. She was visiting Mexico for a few days and next thing you know, they were moving to the good old United States for good." She laughed. "I'm a true citizen."

Sir Bob scribbled a few words in his memo to make it look official.

"Tell me about how you came to own and operate a half-way house." He said. She bumped the ash off her slim cigarette and sighed.

"What can I say?" She paused. Her eyes filled with tears. "I fell in love with a military man." She admitted. She reached over and got a tissue from the dispenser. "We used to talk about owning our own business, buying a house and living the true American dream."

"If this is painful, we can stop." Sir Bob said. "It is never my intention to make a pretty lady cry."

He felt that a statement like that should cheer up any lady her size. She smiled. "It's okay. What is your name again?" She asked, touching his arm.

"You can call me Bob." He told her.

She tried to stand up. Two minutes later, she was on her feet. Sir Bob stopped scribbling and re-lit his cigar.

"I'm sorry, Bob. I try not to get sentimental. It's been such a long time ago. My husband, Cedric Johnson was in the Persian Gulf War. We met and married before he was sent to fight. We had all the ideas and plans of any young couple." She paused. "He was shot and killed. I got the insurance money. I and my sister stayed in the States. She was supposed to help me run this place, but she fell in love with some small class pimp. Charles Patrick Funk. I'll never forget him and he better hope I never find him. He knocked her up and took off six months later. Never to be heard from again."

Sir Bob was now getting somewhere. He scribbled the name Charles Patrick Funk in his memo and began to ask questions.

"I'm so sorry." He placed an arm around her shoulder and tried to comfort her. "How did she make out?" He asked. Momma Lou slowly wobbled back to her desk and got the bottle of Tequila and two more glasses. When she made it back to the table, she poured them another drink.

"I'm gonna call for lunch for us. Will that be okay?" She asked, while handing him the glass.

"Yes." He answered.

"Please, may I treat you?" He asked her.

She pulled a menu from her pocket. "I'm gonna have the ham and cheese combo. What would you like?" She asked him. She gave him the menu. Sir Bob quickly saw a Rubin combo and pointed to it.

Momma Lou picked up the phone and placed the order. When she was done, she returned to the table.

"My sister gave birth to a son. Emiliano Patrieko Funk. My first born nephew. Mi papi had strong genes (she smiled). Emiliano came out looking one hundred percent Mexican. My sister gave him papi's name, Emiliano." Finally, Sir Bob began to feel that his trip to this crime-infested town was going to pay off. Although he never really doubted Mrs. Matty's advice, he wasn't sure where she was leading him and why. He suddenly had a feeling it was all about to come together like one giant jigsaw puzzle.

"How did your sister make out as a single parent?" Sir Bob asked again. "She was fine." Momma Lou continued.

"I helped support her. I gave her some of my settlement and she invested half of it in a fund for Emiliano. We paid for private school until he was twelve years old. By then, he was fluent in Spanish and English. The invested funds matured and paid well. When he turned thirteen, he announced that Emiliano was an old fashioned name and he wanted to be called Patreiko. That's when all the trouble started with him." She shook her head. "Trouble?" Sir Bob asked.

"Patreiko kept finding trouble." She told him. "He grew to be a tall handsome young man, but apparently, he took after his good for nothing father." She frowned.

Momma Lou filled their glasses with more tequila. Sir Bob didn't usually drink anything other than Absinthe, especially while working, but alcohol was making her talk and he listened, wanting to hear more.

"He kept getting in trouble." She added. "He had a couple close friends. They ran the streets calling themselves The P-Funk Gang."

"Bingo!" Sir Bob accidentally yelled out loud. "He smiled and quickly looked at his empty shot glass as a cover.

Momma Lou laughed. "It's hitting you good now, ain't it, amigo?" Sir Bob smiled.

"Tell me more about your nephew's gang. This is interesting stuff. I mean to find out about the heritage and gut root of the establishment as well as the lovely dame behind it."

Momma Lou covered her blushing face with her hands, showing her double spare tire of a midsection. One of the tenants came bursting through the door as if he was in some kind of happy rage.

"Momma Lou, has the mail come yet?" He asked, all wild wild-eyed. He was constantly moving, as if he had to urinate. He sniffed his fingers and licked his lips like there was leftover glaze frosting on them.

"Not yet La'won." She replied. "Have you been out looking for work today?"

"Yes ma'am. I went out dis morning." He told her. He dashed out of the lobby toward the rooms. The food finally arrived and Sir Bob handed her a twenty twenty-dollar bill.

"He can keep the change." He announced.

Momma Lou took the money and met the young delivery boy half way. She grabbed the container, gave him the money, and headed back to the table. The boy smiled excitedly and ran out the door with a three dollar tip. Momma Lou grabbed the Tequila and mixed it in with her cola, then offered it to Sir Bob, who passed. As she ate, she began to elaborate more about her nephew.

"Patreiko had money to live on and pay his bills. My sister made sure of that. She told him to go to work, make his own money, for pleasures." She put a few fries in her mouth. "He was spoiled. Twenty years old, he was and wanted to hang out with his friends all day and do nothing. One day, he was standing on the porch and three little economy cars were delivered to him from Mexico. We didn't know where they came from. Patrieko said he bought them.

Sure enough, he had the titles." She bit into the sub sandwich. "He later admitted that he had been gambling and won so much money. He wanted the P-Funk gang to be exquisite.

Later that week, we found drugs in his bedroom. My sister, Gabriela put him out the next day. Then he started getting arrested. He and his gang would cruise the streets in those shiny little cars. They'd race each other. He started selling hash. He got arrested a third time and, on a plea deal, he had to attend and complete at least one class over at the Community College. He chose a business class, claiming it would help him get his business off the ground." She took another bite and Sir Bob jotted down interesting parts of her conversation, hoping that by the time she sobered up some, he'd have all the information he needed. He sipped his cola and took a bite.

"Simply delicious." He told her and smiled. She nodded while sipping her mixed drink. "Did college help Patreiko?" Sir Bob asked.

"Helped him to get into more trouble." She said. "He, Jojo and Boogee were working on a plan to rob the pawn shop. They needed a look-out. The judge had already told all of them that if they are in his courtroom again, someone would pay. Boogee had a list of petty thefts for years. Jojo had been caught several times on possession with intent to sell." She noticed Sir Bob writing quickly in his memo pad.

"All of this is simply what I heard after the fact." She told him. "I can't swear to anything.

"It's just as good. I'm not going to put anything personal in the story. I just love hearing about the lives of others." He told her.

"Well, when Patreiko was going to Community College, he was twenty-one years old. That year, the public school system started bussing in High School students to take one two- hour class a day. When Gabriela heard about that, she didn't like it. She often said they shouldn't mix grown ups and children. Patreiko went to visit his mom after the class one day, He drove up in his little economy sports car, with shining spinning rims. An older guy was there trimming the hedges. He saw the car and started asking several questions. He wasn't too old, but a few years older than Patreiko. It was clear that he wanted to make some quick money." She snapped her fingers together. "He was the one who got the worst of it all." "What do you mean?" Sir Bob asked, taking the last bit of his sandwich.

"The judge said he was the oldest one; he should've had enough sense to walk away or try and talk them out of the robbery. Once he knew Patreiko had money and didn't have any trouble getting more. He became one of the boys. Patreiko once gave him five hundred dollars cash, just so he'd have money in his pocket. Ever since then, when Patreiko called, that boy jumped."

"Did he go to the college too?" Sir Bob asked, while lighting a cigar. Momma Lou laughed.

"He wasn't trying to waste time going to another school when he barely managed getting out of high school."

"Patreiko got in trouble at the College?" Sir Bob asked. He crossed his legs and cleared his throat. He had been here with Momma Lou quite a while and he was getting tired, but her story had very interesting information and was hitting on all of Mrs. Matty's leads.

"Well, he met one of the high school girls there. She had a hot name. I can't quite remember it. It was quite unusual." She told him. "He started spending money on her. She kept hanging around him. At first, he thought it was because he was older. He was twenty-one and had a car and his own place.

One day after class, he told her he had to go home cause he was hosting a poker party with his friends. They'd been dating; I guess you can say, for about a month at this point. The little girl asked if she could come over and be the entertainment." She winked at Sir Bob. "She told him that she could use the experience. Claiming a business venture of some sort.

Patreiko was growing fond of her, even though she was six years younger.

He didn't understand about the business venture until he let her come over."

She put the sandwich wrappings in the bag and took another sip of the liquid mixture. Sir Bob closed his memo pad and listened.

"This lil lady showed up with a portable stripper pole. Installed it in the living room where they were playing poker. She slipped into a two two-piece leather bikini type outfit, put a cassette tape in the radio, and started pole dancing." She told him, while laughing and starting to sweat. Several tenants ran in and out of the lobby while she sat there, slapping her leg and laughing wildly.

"She got started early, did she?" Sir Bob commented.

"That's not all." She told him. "One of those boys told the judge everything, trying to stay out of jail. Unfortunately, the judge had had enough and was hard on him. He was 25.

"Did anyone stop the girl from dancing?" Sir Bob asked.

Momma Lou smiled. "She wanted experience. There were three intoxicated guys drinking, smoking and playing poker in the same room. When she took a break from dancing, the older one asked Pateiko how much for personal service. He told him a hundred bucks for him plus her fee. He paid for it and went to the other room. Thirty minutes later, when he got back, the other one paid up and left out with her for an hour or so. It was one after the other. Then, mi sobrino got a little jealous and decided he really liked her, so he was ready for his turn. They were all so drunk at this point, that they just sat there looking. The boy said that Patreiko looked at her and told her to go take a shower. About thirty minutes later, she turned off the water and called to him to bring her a towel. He had clean laundry in the living room. By this point, no one could stand straight and he told her to come get it herself. She got a little upset and stormed into the living room dripping wet, bend over and started digging for a towel.

Then he said Patrieko got up grabb her by the arm and pushed her on the couch. At first, the boy said, she yelled at him that he hadn't paid for any of that. The others just watched.

Patreiko had to prove in front of his gang that he was always in charge of things.

He called the shots and he came first. When it was all over, he whispered in her ear that he would take her shopping that weekend." She paused. "I'm his aunt. I can't say if he would do that or not. All I know is that he went down the wrong road soon after his thirteenth birthday."

Sir Bob sat there for a second, trying to digest his food and inhale the full story. Spicey's full story. New things he didn't know about her. Things he wasn't sure he wanted to know   about her.

He cleared his throat. "What happened with the little girl?" He asked curiously.

Momma Lou leaned back in the chair. It creaked loudly but, Sir Bob ignored it since, it didn't break.

"Patreiko kept his word." She said. "He liked the girl, but she made him pay that weekend. He spent nearly four hundred dollars on her. She made him buy makeup, night gowns, dresses, purses and high heel shoes and cologne. I think they said when he got back home, he had $75.00 left and she took $50.00 of that." She told him.

Sir Bob looked at her, nearly in shock. "She didn't report the rape?" He asked.

"She was fifteen. She liked Patreiko and she didn't want to get him in trouble. She didn't want to get in trouble either. A few days later, the rumor of the rape flooded the neighborhood. People began to talk. After that, Patreiko was busted on a mall parking lot selling hash. He was in jail for two weeks.

When he got out, the little girl showed up at his apartment, asking for money for an abortion.

Patrieko refused and asked her to marry him. They argued for a while and she left. A month later, he and his gang got arrested for a series of arsons and robbing a pawn shop not too far from here. That's when the older boy got twenty years for being a look out for the others. One of the boys ran into the girl, a year or so later and she told them she took care of it. Patreiko was upset because he didn't want her to get an abortion. He supposedly told her that he'd get even some day. A few days later, he went on a personal rage cutting tires, setting fires, breaking windows, etc. He got arrested again and reunited breifly briefly with his older buddy. He was released on bail and went back to Mexico. I think." She said.

"All of what I say is what I heard in the courtroom." She smiled.

"So your business was a dream of yours and through everything that happened within your family, you still managed to get and keep it going." Sir Bob said. He stood, took Momma Lou by the hand, kissed it as he did before, and thanked her for her time.

CLUB CRYSTAL

8:00pm

"Welcome to The Beatnik." The bouncer said, as he smiled and held the door open. Sir Bob nodded appropriately and walked inside. It was an old old-style joint, a little larger than a run-down hole in the wall. Apparently, a social hot spot for the older population who enjoyed a few drinks, snacks and maybe a live performance or two. He made his way to a vacant table, in the middle of the room, and sat down. He was soon greeted by a waitress as she handed him the nightly program along with a menu.

"You look like a drifter, so I'll tell ya how thangs go here, if you care to know." She said to him. Sir Bob smiled at her, glad to know that he'd choose the right ragged attire to keep them from guessing his true occupation. He was two days unshaven and had tossed his hair around just enough to give it an uncombed, tangled look. His stained overcoat was one that he'd picked up from the local third third-hand store for a couple bucks. It was already brown, so the stains didn't really show unless you just starred.

"Okay, so here what we got." The waitress announced. "Fried chicken, fried Catfish, a big ole chef salad, if you wanna eat healthy and shit. We also offer nachos, chips and free popcorn."

About that time, another waitress arrived and placed a paper bucket of popcorn on the table and walked away.

"We got beer, whiskey, cola and ginger ale.

"(She paused) "Tonight is poetry night. Our featured poet is Tashawanna. Would you like a moment to look over the menu and choose what you want?"

"Yes, please." Sir Bob replied, trying to sound as American as he could.

"You ain't gotta be so nice honey; we get a lot of white folk in here every night. They'll be here after the band arrives and then the place stort jumpin'." She assured him. Sir Bob smiled appreciatively.

Walking away, she turned towards him one last time.

"By the way, the featured artist usually does two performances per night. Just a repeat for the folks who missed it earlier." She added.

Some of the lights dimmed and a four four-man band gathered on stage. Each one, drumming and strumming random beats and chords. The bar was still noisy, so Sir Bob considered this a warm

warm-up session for them as he enjoyed his popcorn and waited for the main event.

A few minutes later a gentleman, in an old styled black and white pinstripe suit appeared on center stage and welcomed everyone to the bar. When he walked away, the spotlight came on and the bar darkened. The only lights in the audience were the night lights on the tables.

The performer made her entrance onto the stage from behind the side curtain. A   particularly rough, haggard haggard-looking dame, she was. Sir Bob looked in amazement at her lean, muscular body. She was ripped, and toned with cat- liklikee features. *"Wouldn't mind hitting that"*, he thought to himself, as he gulped down the last of the house beer he'd undoubtedly mixed with absinthe. As the liquor began to overcome the beer, his senses strengthened and suddenly, he was sitting there about to watch the stage performance while listening closely to all the conversations around him. He was able to hear without straining, as if he was there at the table with each person. He secretly prided himself at how well he could zone out while still working a case and still come out on top. He had been doing it since he was a teen-age super sleuth, solving minor neighborhood crimes, back in Brisbane during the mid-seventies. He paused to reminisce a bit about strolling around the Mount Coot-tha trails with his best friends, hoping to pick up college girls, when a burst of laughter and clapping snapped him back into the reality. He put a handful of popcorn into his mouth and focused on the stage. The performer had her back to the audience in a frozen type of pose that gave the onlookers no choice but to focus on her plump, protruding backside. Yet, the angle, shape and the way of the pose was extreme and led Sir Bob to look a little deeper than what he saw. As the musicians began to play some kind of funky   rhythm in accelerated four-four time, the performer twirled around on her feet and threw her hands in the air, as she introduced herself.

"Tashawanna!" She said, while fluttering her extra extra-long lashes to the crowd and licking her large, dry painted lips seductively. They were as plump and round as her backside. The more popcorn Sir Bob ate, the more revealing the performer became, but he was not ready for this just yet. Feeling slightly baffled, he waved his hand in the air and the waitress returned to fill his glass with another round of house beer. Lighting a cigar, he gulped down some beer then added a good splash of liquor to his mug and listened. On the other side of the room, three partially drunk men sat together speaking of a job they held when they were younger. They mentioned the old factory, four blocks away that had a "now hiring" sign dangling out front, offering above minimum wage pay. Sir Bob listened closely. He was splitting up his attention between the performing artist on stage and conversations around the room. With his mixed drink and cigar, he managed this task just fine.

"Sisko whatever happen wit dat lil ole gal you was so in love wit back den." One guy asked with a cigarette dangling from his lips.

"His old ass madd dat gal mane." The other man answered quickly.

"Watcho malf now. Ain no dead old mane." Sisko said happily. He smiled devilishly and took a shot of liquor before chasing it with a half mug of beer. The bald friend slapped his hand onto his knee and laughed wildly. "I tollya he wuzzn' lettin' dat getaway." He growled out. His fat neck obviously made him short of breath as he barely completed the sentence while laughing.

"See, see you tawk too much Baia." Sisko teased him. " You can run yo malf up to Yew Yalk and back fasta than the speed of light." Sisko told him. Baia was still laughing. His stomach bumped aganist the table, making it shake, as the liquid jiggled about in the steins.

Sir Bob took another puff of his cigar and gazed at the ceiling. The three gentlemen continued their conversation as the audience laughed, clapped and commented on the performer's"s actions as she bellowed out such a hard force of words.

Her hatred was almost unfeminine-like, a bit inhumane, but they touched the heart of the audience. What it was about this lady was unclear to Sir Bob. All he was sure of, was that his earlier opinion was beginning to fade just as quickly as ice in a deep fried potato.

Perhaps it was the popcorn that was making him see her differently. He took another sip of his mixed alcohol and listened closely while catching the eye of the poet. She smiled at him, in a meet me around back kind of way, pausing and displaying a duck-mouth freeze freeze-frame as if she was waiting for verification from him. He cleared his throat and quickly looked away, nodding a friendly hello to a couple as they passed by his table. He could still hear the conversation of the three older gentlemen. It was apparent that they were playing a card game of some sort.

"Three kangs!" One of them called out, while slapping the cards onto the table.

"Baia gotchu dare Sisko." The bald guy confirmed. "Ahh, lagg ain't did nuttin'." Sisko replied.

"Three aces!" Sisko called out proudly.

Sir Bob removed a small memo pad from his breast pocket and scribbled the names Lagg, Baia and Sisko on it. He wasn't sure why, but he did just because these names presented themselves in this little performing bar setting.

He glanced upon the stage just in time to see the finishing spin and close of the act. The poet once again, announced a name, posed and froze briefly in place. The crowd gave a standing ovation. When they began to sit down, Sir Bob noticed the long flowing hair of the poet. It was red. It was as red as the strand of fiber back at his hotel room. He rushed to get closer to her but was constantly blocked by patrons getting up and moving about. By the time he'd made his way to the bottom of the stage, she had disappeared behind the curtain, just as elaborately as she had appeared. Disappointed, he returned to his table, pulled out his memo pad and added the name "Tashawanna." He Sighed heavily and ordered a fresh mug of beer while re-lighting his cigar.

Sir Bob quickly excused himself and dashed around back, trying to find that interesting poet. She dashed in and out of alleyways and up stairways until finally reaching a back door, all decorated in flashing blue lights. Sir Bob waited outside for a few minutes before clenching his dillinger, knocking twice and turning the doorknob.

The poet stood in front of the mirror that was barely hanging onto the wall above the small sink.

It was an efficiency room. The extra long twin size bed was next to the wall, below the small window. Next to the door was a plaque to hang your keys and a three feet metal rod structure for hanging clothes. The toilet was hidden inside a small closet with three shelves placed above it. There was barely enough room to stand and adjust your clothes after relieving yourself, but it was cheap and close to the club. It was home.

Tashawanna applied the mascara to her eyelashes with slow, precise strokes. Paying careful attention to her appearance. Satisfied with the right eye, she blinked twice while sucking in her cheeks to see what it would look like once she was all made up and on stage. Before she could start on the other lash, there was a knock on the door. The forcefulness of the bang made the hanging light in front of the mirror swing a little. She sighed and responded to the knock.

"Come in,"she yelled over her shoulder. Sir Bob cautiously, turned the doorknob and pushed the door open. He waited in anticipation before entering. The lady got a glimpse of his hand and turned around.

"Come on in honey. I don't got all day. What can I do you for.?" She asked and winked. Her voice was smooth with a certain kind of "something" about it.

Sir Bob stepped inside and immediately closed the door. "Tashawanna, I presume." He said.

She looked him over, with the mascara tube in her hand, and sucked in her cheeks. Once again, giving an instant duck-mouth look.

"Yes." She answered. "I have a show in two hours, so if you want it, make it quick, and from the looks of you, it's gonna be at least a $200.00 deal. I need to finish my makeup first."

"Oh, please, by all means, carry on." Sir Bob responded. "I'm really not here for um, that." He told her.

Tashawanna looked up at him, in the mirror, and continued to apply the mascara to the other side. She blinked twice and began to apply eyeshadow.

"So why are you here honey?" She asked. "I know you from somewhere?" She stepped away from the mirror with her back to him and adjusted the half grapefruit rhine inside her bra. They made her breast look perky and firm at all times and she loved it.

It was a trick she had picked up years ago. Buy a grapefruit, cut it in half, gut out the halves and place it over the chest bumps. Instant soft boobs with a natural citrus smell as well.

"Well, I saw your act and got a little curious. That's all." Sir Bob told her.

"That's some kind of curious for a guy not to want all dis." She replied while creating a motion of waves with her body. "I got the bag of chips too. You know what I mean?" She winked.

CHOCOLATE COCOA DIVA

I got my hair hooked up tight.

I got my makeup just right.

I'm wearing my pink wig,

you know, the one that I like.

Wearing my short dress,

that barely covers my thighs,

When men see me,

they get all bug eyed.

Hmph!

Chocolate Cocoa Diva!

My breast are perky, and

welcoming y'all.

My nice lil fluid-filled jiggly balls.

That's one way to pay the bills,

turning them tricks,

in six inch heels.

Ahh!

Ain't no shame,

it's part of the game,

Ignore the chronic psychological strain.

Feed off the one,

who caused the pain.

Keep shaking that booty,

and making it rain.

Chocolate Cocoa Diva!

JESS LIKE DAT PRODUCTIONS

Sir Bob reached into the backseat to retrieve his briefcase. Sliding off the top was a neon pink and black laminated calling card that read: "*Sexie A. Butt. Personal Entertainer*" He thought back to his meeting with Macklewayne. The smile the trucker displayed, told him that he was indeed expected to call this dame. Maybe not for the reason intended, but Sir Bob would definitely call. Almost immediately, he recalled someone mentioning that Sexie, one of Spicey's dancers, conveniently disappeared the day of the discovery. Sir Bob had a need to contact Sexie Butt. He sat peacefully for a moment to clear his mind and relax   before continuing on. In days of old, his grandmother would often tell him, "*Don't forget to breathe Bobby. It frees the mind.*" He lit a cigar and savored the memory of his unexpected visitor the previous evening. He smiled, curling up the ends of his neatly trimmed mustache. Removing an ancient flip phone from the arm rest compartment, he sighed and placed a call to Sexie.

The phone rang three times and was answered by, what sounded like, an old tired woman. "If you're calling for Sexie, she's busy right now. Current, estimated wait time is five to ten minutes. You wanna hold?" She asked.

"With pleasure." Sir Bob responded. Within seconds, sultry, jazz music began to play. Sir Bob found it quite soothing. He reclined his chair and waited patiently.

Several minutes later, a voice came over the phone. "Dis Sexie." She announced.

"Hello Sexie, my name is Sir Bob. I'm an investigator from Australia. I would like to meet with you to discuss an incident that happened at Spicey's Hangout." He told her.

"I don't work at the Hangout." She notified him. "Iown know nothing."

"Ms. Butt, I am aware that you no longer work at the hideout. I understand you quit suddenly. If you are indeed innocent, of any involvement in the crime, you should meet with me to clear your name of any suspicion." He alerted her. "right now, while everything is being investigated by local officials, with your disappearance, you will be hauled in immediately, once they track you down.

Either you let me help you, or you're going down." He explained. There was a brief silence on the phone. Sir Bob could hear her breathing. She was trying to hide the fact that she was afraid.

Whispering, she told him, "You gonna have to come where I am." "I have no problem with that. Where are you, love?" Sir Bob asked.

"I might be busy when you get here. You will have to wait until after my shoot." She told him. "Where do you work?" He asked.

"I work at Jess Like Dat Productions." She told him. "I'm a model."

Sir Bob scribbled the name of the company on a piece of paper along with her name. "When you get here, ask for Bic Hardcastle. I work for him." She said.

Sir Bob wasn't sure if he'd heard the name Hardcastle before or not, but, with Sexie now working as a model for him, could he have met her at the Hangout? He added Hardcastle to his list and entered Jess Like Dat Productions into his GPS.

The GPS took him on a long ride down the highway nearly an hour or so away from Crystal Town.

For the next forty forty-five minutes, there was nothing but open land. He made a right turn onto a side street that took him into a seemingly wooded area. He saw a sign with a finger pointing left, with the word "STUDIO" written in bold letters. On a hunch, he turned left and was greeted by four men dressed in solid black jeans and gray tee-shirts. They were wearing classic old west style shoulder holsters with what looked like 45 magnums, clearly visible. Sir Bob stopped the car and kept his hands on the steering wheel as one approached him.

"You got business here, compadre?" the man asked sternly. "This is private property." "I do, my good man." Sir Bob answered. "I'm here to see Sexie Butt."

"Visitors, for the models, go through Bic Hardcastle. You got a pass confirmation?" He asked. "No Sir, I don't." Sir Bob responded. "I'm not that kind of visitor." He smiled friendly. "Wait here." He told him as he returned to the other three. They spoke quietly among themselves and looked blankly at his car. One removed a phone from his back pocket and made a phone call. Bob was sure he was alerting Hardcastle of his arrival. Hopefully, Sexie had given word that he was stopping by.

The muscular guy, who made the phone call nodded twice, and fist fist-bumped the short bald one who made his way to the car window.

"Proceed through the gate and make a sharp right. Drive slow or you'll miss your turn. Two miles down the road, you will see four more security guards who will direct you to the studio." He directed.

Sir Bob nodded and proceeded as directed. As he drove down the dirt road, he admired all the different scenes he passed along the way. There was a building that looked like an old general store, a closed down gas station and three small models of houses. It was a real staged neighborhood. Not realizing how far he'd driven, he was soon stopped by more security guards. These appeared more friendly than the first group. They showed him where to park while making small talk about his car.

Soon, Sir Bob entered the Studio. It looked like a waiting room at the doctor's office, except for the erotic pictures on the walls. Sir Bob sat down and waited.

A few minutes later, a tall, dark dark-haired Italian looking guy walked in. "I'm Bic Hardcastle. I hear you're here to speak with one of my girls." He said.

"Yes, Yes, I am." Sir Bob replied, while giving him a quick overview. "Very nice place you have here, my good man." Hardcastle smiled.

"Would you like to come back to the set?" He asked. "Sexie is just about finished with her scene."

"Oh, no, I don't want to interrupt her." Sir Bob told him.

"No such thing. I will show you around. By the time we get to the set, she should be waiting for you in her dressing room." Hardcastle told him. He signaled for Sir Bob to follow him down a dimly lit narrow hallway. Sir Bob clinched his Dillinger as he trailed behind him. He entered a small room that had a display case with several boxes around it.

"This is part of our souvenir shop." Hardcastle told him. "If you're in the market for such items; several of these things I had specially made. Our fans spot them immediately while viewing our movies."

Sir Bob smiled and looked around timidly.

"Let me show you some of our sets that are clear right now." Hardcastle said. He went back out into the hallway and walked around a small spiral staircase. "Nothing up there really, except my office, the doctor's office and a dumbwaiter." Sir Bob slowed his pace.

"A doctor's office?" He asked. "Here?"

"Well, gotta make sure my girls are healthy, ya know? I'm not trying to get anyone sick." He said. "It's just part of the business. I call in a doctor every two weeks to make sure all is well. Besides that, he supplies the contraceptives at a low price."

They walked a few steps and passed by a table that held two ten ten-gallon containers. Oddly enough, one said, "water water-based"," the other, "silicone silicone-based." Next to it was a wall mounted, antibacterial gel dispenser. Mint scented with aloe.

"Oh, you've got to see the wardrobe room." Hardcastle smiled. "Just looking at some of these outfits on the mannequins will make you want a cigarette." He teased. Sir Bob looked around at all the anatomically correct mannequins and wished he could duck out somewhere and take a quick swig of absinthe. Hardcastle looked at his watch. "Ahha! Sexie should be done now." He said.

"How did you manage to get Sexie to work for you?" Sir Bob blurted out as they walked swiftly to the elevator.

"Oh, it took some work with her." He replied. "She was all wrapped up servicing some old rich guy."

Sir Bob hesitated, trying not to cause suspicion. "Rich guys get all the girls, heh?"

"Well." Hardcastle smiled. "Rich or hung. One or the other." They entered a small room where the receptionist sat. Judging from the ashtray on the desk and the beer cans in the trash, Sir Bob could safely assume whoever sat here, was the one answering the phone.

"You can wait here." Hardcastle said, while pointing to a couch pushed up against the wall. "I'll get Sexie for you." Sir Bob winced and smiled. A few minutes later, a skinny, wrinkled older lady came and sat behind the desk. She lit a cigarette and opened a can of bottled beer. "Okay, handsome', she said with the same grisly voice he'd heard over the phone,' what part are you here for?"

"Oh, no, no. I'm not here for any part. I'm waiting to speak with someone." Sir Bob replied. "Oh, a shy one, who doesn't wanna discuss sexual matters with women." She said, looking him over. "That's okay, honey. "Hardcastle will be out in a moment. I never will understand your type. You wanna screw anything in a dress but, when you get here, you're afraid to speak up."

Not commenting, Sir Bob cleared his throat and smiled. The receptionist drank down some beer and started typing.

"I hear you've got a bit of an accent. That might get you extra pay eventually." She told him. "The girls seem to like men with accents in this line of work." She opened the drawer and took out a small bottle of pain relievers. After glaring at it for a second, she shook two or three into her hand and threw them in her mouth, followed by a swig of beer.

Glancing once again at Sir Bob, she leaned back, donned a pair of reading glasses, and started thumbing through a mini mini-mag of some sort. After what seemed like an eternity, a young lady with long pink hair emerged from behind the center door. She was wrapped in a knee knee-length bathrobe and appeared extremely nervous. Her eyes shifted all around the room and out the windows.

"Tammy, you got a couple beers handy?" she asked the receptionist. The receptionist pointed over to a mini mini-fridge. "Help yourself honey." Tammy responded. The young lady grabbed a couple beers and walked over to Sir Bob.

"You here to see Sexie Butt?" she asked him quietly, her voice shaking worse than an alcoholic going through detox.

"Yes, I am." Sir Bob replied.

"That's me." She admitted, while handing him a bottle of Raging Bronco beer. "You wanna talk someplace private?" She asked. Sexie walked quickly out into the hallway, pausing briefly, to wait for Sir Bob.

As he approached, she wrapped her arms around her stomach, keeping her oversized bathroom closed.

"Imma take you to my dressing room." She told him while walking to the end of the hallway. "That's fine." Sir Bob told her. "This shouldn't take long.

Finally, they reached a red door with black stars going around the frame. There was a big star in the center of the door that bore her name. They walked inside. There was a vanity and a mirror, with light bulbs going all around the frame. To the right, on the left wall was a thick, cushioned futon with a day bed next to it. In the corner, there were several cardboard boxes describing the garments inside. In the back of the room, there was a small spiral staircase.

The same type he passed by earlier while walking around with Hardcastle. It was clear that he had direct access to her dressing room. There was also a tiny bathroom with a toilet, shower, and wash basin in the corner. Sexie ushered Sir Bob over to the daybed and offered him a seat.

Sir Bob politely declined and rolled over the chair from the vanity. Sexie, scared to death, didn't say a thing as she sat nervously on the daybed.

"Dey send you to arrest me?" She finally asked.

Sir Bob got a little suspicious and began to keep an eye on the top of the staircase. He rubbed his hand down the left side of his vest, feeling for his Dillinger.

"Why should I arrest you, Love." He asked. "Are you guilty of something?" Sexie shifted and began to perspire.

"Look, ain have no money okay?" She confessed. "I knew dey had warrants out for me. I said I was gonna pay dem tickets and I am. I just didn't need no police interfering wit me right den. I had medical stuff I really needed to take care of, ya know? I couldn't do dat from no jail cell."

Sir Bob listened closely, trying to understand what she was rambling about.

"Bic is a regular at The Hideout. He go there all the time looking for girls to be in his productions. He had been asking me to work for him since the first time he saw my act." Now, Sir Bob had his questions about Hardcastle. However, he appeared and somewhat answered without opening his mouth. He tilted his head to the left and Sexie appeared to hold her breath.

"Calm down, Love." Sir Bob told her. "I'm not here to arrest you. I just want to know what you know about Clarksdale Longstreet.

"You aint tryin' to arrest me?" She asked. "Furreal?"

Sir Bob took a deep breath and removed his flask from his vest pocket and took a swig. He figured that this action alone would prove to her that he wasn't like the typical   investigators she was used to. He didn't mind drinking on the job as long as you don't lose your head in the process.

"I prefer to make my own mixed drinks, if you don't mind." He said and smiled. "Have a taste. Maybe this will help you calm down a little quicker than beer." He offered, handing her his flask.

Sexie let her guard down a little. She smiled and accepted his flask. She watched as Sir Bob lit his cigar, tasted the flavored smoke and blew it smoothly into the air. Her bathrobe fell open slightly and Sir Bob could see a small colorful tattoo on the inside of her left thigh.

Sexie kept her eyes on him as she turned up the container, while Hardcastle watched from around a corner. As the rich golden liquid flowed down upon her tongue and down her throat, she closed her eyes tightly, and swallowed. When she removed the flask from her lips, she handed it back to Bob and smiled shyly.

"I saw Cloggsdale everything Saturday night just about." She admitted. "He was a nice man who paid me well." She shifted on the daybed. "He always gave me at least two hundred dollars, no matter what." She paused for a moment. "I guess his wife just wasn't doing it for him."

"Doing what?" Sir Bob asked. He removed the notepad from his pocket and focused on her deep brown eyes.

"What are you saying girl?" Sir Bob asked, blowing smoke out of the corner of his mouth. "You know." She said. "Hell, everybody know. I did thangs for him and he paid me fudd". She admitted.

Sir Bob scribbled in his notepad and looked back at her. "You offered him services?" Sir Bob said. Sexie squirmed.

"Well, he didn't like coming in the Hangout dat much, so I told him I'd come out. All the other girls had a special spot on the grounds if dey clients wanted to go outside. So I didn't see nothin' wrong wit it." She told him.

"Did you see him the night before he was discovered?" Sir Bob asked.

"I saw him." She held her head down. "We were in the cau; I did my thang, you know? He like did it." She started to day dream a little, looking off in the distance. "Ole Cloggsdale would turn the radio on and we would listen to the hottest baddest hip hop on air. We'd sit there tawkin' and, gettin' thangs stirred up. I'd entertain him, do my job and shit." She smiled. "I was gone in an hour or two." She remembered. She took a sip of the beer. Sir Bob could see that the absinthe was relaxing her, so he reached into his vest pocket and offered her more.

Sexie took the flask, took a good hardy swig and returned it to him. Sir Bob smiled, satisfied that he would get the information he needed. As the alcohol took eaffect, Sexie began to loosen up. She stood up, removed the robe and walked over to the vanity.

Sir Bob looked at her, admiring her plump, proportioned body. She saw him in the mirror and turned around.

"I'm sorry, but I do have another shoot when you leave and, I have to get ready." She told him. Sir Bob ignored her comment and continued his interrogation.

"Did you do anything different that night?" He asked her. "Anything at all"? Sexie picked up a hair brush and started brushing her long pink weave.

"Nope, nothing." She said. "I took care of him as usual. Before he left, he asked me to go get him some peanuts or something. He had a hard blow and was feelin' a lil weak afterwards. I went inside and Bic saw me. We stawded tawkin'. I grabbed my phone and texted Cloggsdale and told him I got tied up and he'd have to get something at the stowe down the road. He replied that he had to sit there for a while before he could drive. He said good night and sent me a kiss emoji."

"You saw Hardcastle?" Sir Bob asked.

"Yeah, I saw him." She admitted. She walked over to Sir Bob and sat on his knee. "Would you brush the back of my hair for me? It's so hard to reach sometimes. Sir Bob took the brush and brushed her long pink hair. He was happy that the alcohol was working, but he knew his limits.

"What did Hardcastle want?" Sir Bob asked ignorantly.

Sexie giggled flirtingly and responded. "Me!" She reached over and grabbed a bottle of massage oil.

"You mind?" She asked, giving the bottle to Sir Bob. He let the cigar burn out and sparingly applied the oil to her shoulders and back. He felt kind of awkward rubbing massage oil on someone he had no interest in, but it was all in the task of a job. Sexie lifted her hair allowing Sir Bob total access to her back. He continued to rub the oil on her back while thoughts of Clara Matty once again flowed in his mind. He was gently stroking her back with the tips of his fingers when a strand of hair fell on his wrist. Feeling it, he looked down to flick it off and recognized the fiber almost immediately. Instantly in his mind he knew, the cause of death was asphyxiation by the weave. Pink weave! The problem was, Sexie was innocent. She didn't kill Longstreet. He gave her money and lots of it, he thought.

"What's wrong Daddy?" Why you stop? Sexie asked him.

"Sexie, are you sure that you're not involved with this in any way?" He asked her.

Sexie finally stood her ground and told him, very directly, that she did not kill Clarksdale. Even though Sir Bob had a strain of her pink weave entangled in his watch, he still had a gut feeling that she wasn't his killer. He needed to get back to his hotel room and match up the fiber in his watch to that found on the car. If Sexie is indeed innocent, he was going to protect her.

"It's been nice talking to you honey. I have all I need." Sir Bob said. He stood up, gave her a partial hug and walked out into the hallway. Hardcastle was walking towards him.

"Did your talk go well?" He stopped to inquire.

"Why yes, it did. Very well," Sir Bob replied. Hardcastle pulled him into a nearby corner, nearly out of sight. Sir Bob positioned his hand to quickly defend himself, if the need arose. "Is she in trouble, man?" He asked. "She's my star girl right now. How much is it going to cost to clear her?" Sir Bob saw nothing but confusing sincerity in his eyes.

"Right now, she's good. That's all I know. I'll keep you informed." He told Hardcastle.

"Here, let me walk you to the door." He said. Sir Bob nodded. "I got the money!" Hardcastle yelled to him as he exited.

Ya boy JoJo caint handle me,

Nawl baby,

I'm more than just another twig on his tree.

He comes to me on bended knee,

giving up that green,

and seeking validity.

I will send 'yo emotions in a hysterical daze,

You'll be calling my name,

on all yo' pay days.

If you got a wife

I will make you lea-va,

Now you dealin wit me,

Chocolate Cocoa Diva

Whew!

PHONE CONVERSATION

(Sir Bob to Spicey)

I can assure you, madam; they will not be shutting you down. You should pack for a little get-a-way when all of this blows over. Maybe a good ole trip to Oz would help. I have a nice place there. We could sit back, relax, throw a few snaggs and chops on the barbie, if you'd like, and watch the HoneyEaters. They love coming into my yard and strolling about. I think it's the bird seed I buy. (he paused)

Oh, your ex-employee is not a suspect with me. she could be, by all rights with the local PD, simply due to the way she fled. Most people with warrants try their best to avoid the police at all cost. Ms. Butt is wanted for not paying parking tickets. A somewhat minor offense if you ask me. They may   try to take her in for a backroom waltz, just to find out what she knows. From what I can tell, she and Longstreet were friends. she provided services and he paid exceptionally well. The girl's no killer. she ran because of unpaid parking tickets. As for her job with you, she figured instead of having to chuck a sickie for several days; she would just quit. After all, Hardcastle had offered her a sweet deal, and fame, as a movie star.

I ran into him as well. He's not the Dag I imagined. He actually runs a very organized operation out in the county. Very well hidden, I might add. If it wasn't for the footpath, one could easily get lost.

By the way, I'm planning a trip back to Crystal Town. While waiting for a taxi, when I was there, I walked next door to get a soda and a scratchy or two. That's when I saw this drongo looking bloke ear-bashing a bouncer at a run-down nightclub of some sort. Something about his tone got my attention. It may be nothing but I got a serious hunch. I think I'm going back to check it out. If the local authorities try to shake you up, just have them call me. I will act as your attorney. As you know, I spoke with a friend of yours. Clara Matty. An A-1 sheila she is! Do you see her often? There was a long pause in the conversation while Sir Bob reminisced and Spicey silently steamed.

We met at the hotel and had a lovely chat in my suite. I'll tell ya. she's no dingbat.

Lovely lady. she's got plenty of sense and a kind, caring, spirit about her. (he paused) she left a list for me before leaving the next morning.

Yes, of course, he was strangled with red synthetic fibers. 5-same color as 5exy's hair. Had local police seen 5exy that day, an A.P. B. would've been issued immediately after they'd searched the car. she would've been sitting in a cell awaiting trail for first first-degree murder.

Across town, Mrs. Matty sat on the porch staring out at the bright morning sun, while drinking her coffee and reflecting on life. On one hand, she could understand why Lillie was so into Notto Slugg, but on the other hand, she tried to block out her thoughts of Sir Bob. It wasn't that she was falling for him. Her mind was just fixated on him and she couldn't understand why. She'd had her share of suitors, and at her age, she had given up on finding anyone who made her happy. Like most people, who had given up on something or another, she became accustomed to relying on old sayings and quotes to get her through.

A *good man is hard to find.* "Ain't dat the truth?" She said to herself.

"Finding a good man is like finding a needle in a haystack. Heen got the good sense God gave him to figure his way out. All he got on his mind is sticking you. Once he do dat, he's gone."

It's not that she hated men, she'd just kind of given up on them, especially after spending a total of 12 years of her life trying to find someone who would make her life complete.

She thought briefly about Beauzelle. The janitor at the old neighborhood grade school. Back when she was younger, she'd hooked up with him and spent four years of her adult life cooking and cleaning and trying to create a happy life for them both. He fussed and moaned about his job all day and every day, while drowning himself in 40 40-ounce bottles of malt liquor after work. If she said anything, it became an all all-day verbal fight that increased her blood pressure and endangered her health. She couldn't watch the 6:00 news without him giving the reason for some criminal to commit a crime. Of course, somehow, it all led back to his job. Before getting rid of him, Mrs. Matty decided she needed a man who kept his work at work. A man who realized that the best way to improve his situation is to improve himself!

"Take a look in dat mirra ova there Bo! You'll find yo problem." She often told him. He'd then burst into some sort of craziness about respecting him, like he'd actually earned some sort of royal crown. It didn't take long for her to realize that his place was right back in the halls of the school, mopping puke off the cafeteria floor and trying to get clogged toilets to flush. He quit that job a short time after they broke up because a teacher made him mad. Mrs. Matty heard he was back home living with his mother.

Then there was Holloway. Ole Holloway worked at the grocery store warehouse, unloading trucks with a forklift and stocking shelves. *"He was some kind of handsome,"* she thought. He was real tall, almost seven feet, she guessed. His muscular arms reminded her of that cartoon man who was always eating a can of greens. He had real smooth skin, a thin pencil line moustache, that he kept real neat and trim, and a goat-tee. His downfall was hanging out at bars and strip clubs. He'd often come home smelling of liquor of dried sex.

"That's my cologne Clara. Dat's how it smell when it drys up. Ain't nobaddy cheatin' on you!" He often lied.

After having about three or four illegitimate kids, Holloway got married and ended up retiring from that job after another dock worker tipped over a forklift. The worker got fired while Holloway got compensation for a crushed ankle that left him walking with a limp.

After that, he stopped running to bars and strip clubs and became a deacon at a church.

That was until he got a couple choir members and a ursher pregnant. His wife eventually left him, but came back when she started missing the money. It was said that she was from a project community on the West side of town so, when she married Holloway, who drove a mechanical machine for a grocery store company, she thought she had hit it big.

When Mrs. Matty began to reminisce about Clearwater Jones, she started to hear squeaking and banging sounds coming from Millie's house next door. Millie's grandson had moved in a few weeks ago and brought constant traffic with him. Through the squeaking of metal springs and coils, Mrs. Matty could hear loud love songs playing on the radio through the raised window.

At first, it spoiled her peacefulness and was beginning to ruin the flavor of her coffee. She reached in the pocket of her robe and pulled out a small bottle of cognac.

She added a nice splash or two to her coffee and the thoughts of Clearwater was resurrected.

She smiled at the thought of him. They had the best time together. Clearwater was the general manager at a hotel where she had worked during her early thirties. Mrs. Matty worked in the laundry room; bleaching bed covers all day long, right next door to Clearwater's office. She'd never known anyone who claimed to be a real American Indian before. Clearwater looked black to her, but said that his mother gave him the name Clearwater to carry on his ancestry from her line. His daddy's name was Eddie Lee Jones. Clearwater claimed he grew up on a reservation until he was 19 and headed off to college. Mrs. Matty didn't believe much of anything he said, but he was intelligent and knew how to hold a conversation. She liked his long back ponytail, although when he let his hair down, he looked like a mangly haired woman by the head.

She and Clearwater had moved in together, unbeknownst to the hotel staff. For a few years, everything was fine until he came home broke as an under bridge bum one day. They had just gotten paid.

Clearwater was a gambler. He got paid big money for managing the hotel and he spent big at gambling holes. Once he started losing, he spent more, claiming that he could once again beat the odds and it would only take a few more hundreds of dollars.

Eventually, she kicked him out, and he took over a room at the hotel until it changed owners. He packed his bags and went home to Oklahoma.

That was then and this was now. Once again, time was rolling on in Clara Matty's life. Her best friend was having a steamy love affair with some wanna be young senior citizen slow rollin' around on a motorcycle, while other mature folks were at home watching, drama drama-filled, made for television movies and wishing all that steamy, hot passion was happening to them. Maybe.

The telephone rang and Mrs. Matty quickly pushed herself up from the gliding rocker and went inside to see who was calling.

"Well I sey. It's Lillie." She said to herself.

"Hey Lillie." She answered. "What you and Notto up to today?" She asked, halfway wanting to tag along, but all she heard was sniffling and blubbering.

"Tell you what Lillie', Mrs, Matty said, 'you juss come on ova here and tell me 'bout it. I can hear you better than". She told her.

An half hour later, Lillie was walking through the door headed for the gossip stool in the kitchen.

"I'own wonna see dat lann tale mane no 'mo, no where, Matty." She cried out between sniffles. "He went and took some ole new 'ho riding up through Gilleylen Pogg on his motorbike. Gonna tell me, he had some errand to run wit his grandboys. My cuttin' Roebel picked me up to go to the stow and there he was turnin' into the pogg. You know where all dem big shade trees and thangs aw? Justa laughin' and grinnin'. Helfa sittin' behind him lookin' like a worn worn-out sea-hagg. Had that yellow and blue hair in her head, like these young folks wear. You know the kind, Matty?" She said.

Mrs. Matty hated the fact that her best friend was hurting, but she sure was glad everything was over between Lillie and Notto Slugg. Now Lillie was free to hang out with her again.

Still, Mrs. Mattie sat patiently and listened attentively to the woes and concerns of her best friend. Not once did she criticize or utter such meaningless words, such as *"I told you so," or "You should've known better."* Instead, she comforted Lillie with an everlasting, endless ear. She never appeared to be bored or not interested. She walked through the house, keeping the tea warm and inviting with a couple splashes of absinthe. Something she had recently acquired a taste for.

Lillie talked and blubbered worse than a schoolgirl on the brinks of maturity. Mrs. Mattie stood there nodding and mixing batter for a batch of her newly famous homemade scones. She had a new recipe she copied from a hotel magazine while visiting Sir Bob. Lillie pulled a tissue from the gold box near the cupboard and dried her tears.

"Mattie, I was starting to care about Slugg." She admitted. "Ain't been so hurt since Strongbo passed on me."

"Strongbo was a good mane." Mrs. Mattie replied, while pouring a splash of milk in the mixing bowl. "Yawl stayed Madd 'bout 25 yeels didntcha? I still memba da day yawl got madd. It sho was a booful salmony. The passa standin' dare in a combination of the colors yawl woe. Folks sangin' dem harmony songs and thangs. Um hmm, I memba." She smiled and nodded attentively.

The tears in Lillie's eyes started to flow as she remembered seeing Slugg.

"You should've seen 'em Matty. Slugg was ridin' 'round in the pogg wit dat hot pants wearing Myrtle. Slug was tyna act all like he a young mane." Lillie told her.

Mrs. Matty's eyes nearly flew out the sockets when her head sprang back in sheer surprise.

"Muddle Jane!?" Mrs. Matty asked. "Dat old skinny halfa who wear them ole different colored Ledda booty shahts all stuck up in the meat house?" Mrs. Mattie frowned her face in disgust, showing age lines upon wrinkles. "That's nasty." She said. Anytime you can smell someone in a room baafo you see em, thangs ain't clean." She said while tilting her head towards the floor. She broke off a chunk of chewing tobacco and stuffed it in her mouth.

"Muddle Jane runnin' ran smellin' like hot piss and muscle rub. I tell you. If he runnin' wit dat, Notto Slugg got Dee-zees!"

"What you talkin' 'bout Mattie?" Lillie asked, sounding a little worried.

Mrs. Mattie refilled Lillie's coffee mug and lowered her voice as if others were listening. "I hudd Muddle askin' dat nuss 'bout gettin' shots once a week fah two months. I thank she caught sump'n wearin' dems tight ass shahts all up in ha tail."

Suddenly, the ladies heard the squealing of tires outside the house. Mrs. Matty rushed as quickly as she could to the living room door.

"Ahh Lahd!" She shouted. "Sumbaddy gone run my house down!"

To her surprise, she saw Stank Stank getting out of a bright orange convertible parked in front of her house. She yelled out to him.

"Boy, has you done lost 'yo damn mind? 'Whadda Hell you tryna do to me? Imma old woman acceptable to hodd attacks and thangs. " She fanned her head and chest, trying to rid herself of sweat beads.

"I'm sorry Mrs. Matty." He said. "I jest had to come see you and tell you what I seen ova in da pogg." He immediately rushed to the door, displaying wide, informative eyes.

Already knowing of his discovery, Mrs. Matty moved him away from the open door and shussed him.

"I got Lillie in here now, baby. She done seed dat two-timing, gray-haired fool. He thank he got him something special with dat old stale ho." Mrs. Mattie told him.

"Aw damn, Mrs. Matty." Stank Stank said apologethically. "A'in know she node 'bout it already. Dat's elfed up." He replied.

Mrs. Matty nodded and gave Stank Stank a lite sideways hug.

"You watch yo malf now baby. You know Mrs. Matty don't like you talkin' like dat. Make folk thank you ain't got nothin' in yo brain." She told him.

"Yes Ma'am." He said.

"Matty who dat 'bout to run yo house down?" Lillie asked. "Ain't dat Notto Slugg tryna drive one dem new spokts cahhs is it?" She asked, while struggling to hold back tears of a broken heart.

"Dis my baby, Stank Stank." Mrs. Matty replied, while winking at him and nodding. Stank Stank received the "Hush" signal loud and clear.

"He came by to have a cup of coffee wit me." She lied. "He always comin' over for a quick second to check on old Mrs. Matty. cCoas you know young folk daday ain't got no time to be sitting ran tawkn'. Dey bees busy tryna get dey stuff on and thangs." Mrs. Matty said.

"Come moan in Baby." She said to him, while holding the screen door open.

Stank Stank walked inside, stepping carefully onto the thick plastic runway covering an   area of the living room carpeting. Lillie emerged from the hallway with a forced smile upon her face.

"Hey Stank." Lillie spoke. "I hudd yo sista looking fa help ova at her work place. She hy anybody yet?" Lillie asked. Stank Stank glanced at Mrs. Mattie.

"On know Mrs. Lillie. Sheen said nuttin' 'bout it lately." He lied.

The news of seeing Notto Slugg with Myrtle Jean wasn't the only thing Stank Stank rushed over to tell Mrs. Mattie. What he wanted to tell her was that Myrtle Jean had applied for a job at Spicey's Hangout and Spicey actually hired her!

Spicey, who considered herself one of the top business women in the area, saw Myrtle jean as being a lot like what she hoped to be like in her golden years when it came to men. Only difference is Spicey hoped to be living in a big fancy mansion, with a huge bank account, several nice cars and a harem of men at her beck and call.

Financially speaking, Myrtle Jean could bring in new customers. Senior men from the senior center with their leather wallets and rolled up dusty socks with perfectly creased old money. It was financial genius in Spicey's eyes.

"I s'pose I better get on back 'round the corna Matty. I was wontin' to baul some butter beans and mawgs today." Lillie announced.

"Omm Mrs. Lillie." Stank Stank wrinkled his forehead and licked his lips. 'If you fixin' some hot cornbread wit all that goodness, I might hafta come by and check on you a lil later. Make sho dat food safe fa ya to eat." He smiled at her and rubbed his stomach in anticipation.

Lillie smiled at Stank Stank and gently squeezed his arm as she walked by.

"I'll call you later Lillie." Mrs Matty told her. "Don't you fall weak to Slugg if he come slithering by." After Lillie was off the porch and on her way, Stank Stank turned to Mrs Matty with widened eyes and made his announcement.

"Mrs. Myrtle Jean workin' for Spicey now!" He blurted out to Mrs. Matty. "Spicey payin' her." Mrs. Matty's head flew back in surprise as her right hand flew across her chest. "What you sey! Dat dirty ole skunk shakin' her dusty tail at the 'ho house at ha age?

Dessa damn shame." Mrs. Matty shook her head in disbelief.

"I need to see dis. Isshee pulling money in?" She asked while flopping down on the couch. She pulled a hunk of snuff from the pocket of her apron and securely stuffed her lip.

"Iown know Mrs. Matty." Stank Stank answered. "Spicey told me she had the hook up with old men. Ain know what she was talkin' bout til she sunt me dis picture rat hure."

Stank Stank pulled a large cell phone from his shirt pocket and showed Mrs. Matty a poster of Myrtle Jean in a two two-piece red leather bikini with a caption that said "Not Old.

Experienced". Mrs. Matty looked at the photo and wrinkled her nose.

"Caincha just smell the stale pee and muscle rub?" She asked Stank Stank, who totally missed the comment due to the fact that he was secretly considering a trial run with Myrtle Jean since there was no chance of him increasing his child count.

"Look at dem ole gray eyes she got. Lookin' just like a ole skanky polecat." Mrs. Matty said. Stank Stank smiled devilishly.

"Some men like older women Mrs. Matty." He told her. Mrs. Matty picked up a paper cup from the coffee table and cleared her cheeks of warm brown liquid, "She gone be shakin' her tail for dollas?" She asked hypothetically. Stank Stank was busy adjusting the screen on his phone, so he could clearly view a tattoo he spotted above the old lady's left breast. He smiled and kept the discovery to himself, but Mrs. Matty had glanced at his phone and saw the colorful image of a single rose.

"Umph, the helfa got moggkins on her. Baby, you may have to get me in to see dis." Mrs. Matty said to Stank Stank. "I'm just curious to see how many men gone won't dat." "Thayne no problem Mrs. Matty. Women folk go in dare all the time." He told her. "Spicey place back in bitness now. Especially since dayne tryna shut hu down no 'mo.""

Mrs. Matty looked at him with conning eyes and smiled.

"Whatchu thankin' 'bout Ms. Matty?" Stank Stank asked curiously. Mrs. Matty spit a cheekful of snuff juice into a nearby cup and grinned.

"Nuttin' for you to worry 'bout." She told him. "You gone and take care of yo' thangs. Mrs. Matty good."

Later that evening, Mrs. Matty set out on a shopping spree. She bought all the major items that she thought a well well-groomed man would wear when going out prowling.

Claiming it was for her nephew, she bought a pair of blue and white checkerboard jeans and a blue button button-down short sleeve shirt. Her size five mens' basketball shoes had the brand name of "Our Wear" in bold print under the image of an African fertility mask. She found a matching checkerboard ball cap and decorative non-prescription eyeglasses. She went three stores down to a costume shop, where she bought a beard and moustache set.

With all her items ready for a visit to Spicey's bar, she walked over to the bus stop, sat patiently on the bench and waited for the next number Seven.

Almost as soon as she rested her tired legs, she was approached by a cologne salesman offering her a bottle of perfume for twenty dollars. Mrs. Matty smiled approvingly and purchased a bottle of Stank Stank's favorite fragrance just before boarding the bus.

She had big plans and felt that everything was finally falling in place.

That evening, Mrs. Matty hailed a taxi and headed over to the hangout to witness, for herself, the rumor of Myrtle Jean working for Spicey.

Sliding through the door, dressed in her best "Cat-Daddy" outfit, Mrs. Matty pressed the stick-on facial hair firmly to her face, making sure it was still in place. She positioned the ball cap in such a way that it set just above her black diamond diamond-cut mens' sunglasses. Finding a dark, quiet corner in the observation room, she slid into a secluded booth and studied everyone.

She saw the white bartender who thought he should be black. He danced around, tossing bottles of liquor into the air and catching them as they fell towards empty glasses lined up for refills. He eyed one of the half-naked performers like she was the whip cream on top of his pie. Mrs. Matty slowly scanned the room, taking in all the familiar and not so familiar smells of food, smoke and sex.

To her dismay, she saw no signs of Myrtle Jean, nor did she smell the familiar aroma that roamed the gaming room of the senior center.

"Hey Diddy." A short chunky, nearly naked lady said. "Can I gitcha sumptn'?" Mrs. Matty looked at her and tried to deepen her voice to match her persona.

"Yea, yea, a um, frosty mug of sumptin." She growled out.

Accidentally on purpose, the waitress dropped a pen on the floor and bent over to pick it up, angling her butt in Mrs. Matty's face. Mrs. Matty fought back words of anger and insult as she immediately looked away.

"So, all you want is a frosty mug and a bowl of free popcorn?" The waitress asked.

Mrs. Matty nodded quickly and pulled a cell phone from her pocket and pretended to take a call. With that, the waitress vanished quickly into the darkness.

"Mrs. Matty?" She heard a voice from the darkness whisper out. 'What the Hell?"

Pulling her ball cap forward a little more as she chewed on a dangling cigar she responded, "Om ManLee Mathis, Iown know ya momma and I ain't ya daddy. Go on now. Leave me be."

She felt the muscles in her body tense up as the dark figure moved towards her. "Mrs. Matty. I know dat's you." The somewhat familiar voice whispered over her shoulder. She lit a match and sneaked a peek. Sitting there in a mass of darkness was Stank Stank with wide-open red red-tinted eyes.

"Whatcha doin' hidin?" She asked him curiously.

"Ain hidin'. I was with Sexy. She always be ackin' skid when she come hure. Like she thank ole Longstreet's ghost gonna jump out and smack her or sump'n. Thank she owe a frew mo' dollas on some poggin' tickets downtown." He told her.

"Now what's yo story?" Stank Stank asked, while twirling a cinnamon-flavored toothpick around his lips.

Mrs. Matty leaned back a little. "Don't get too close to me. We men folk". She reminded him. Stank Stank smirked at her through tipsy eyes and awaited her story.

"I wonted to see for myself what Muddle Jane doin' in dis place. Lillie was s'pose to come with me but she had to call dem stumma-nators out to spray. Said she seeing dem ole devilish rorches all ova da house. Claim she even seed a few of dem 'lil fat thangs that leave slob on da flo."

The waitress returned with a bowl of popcorn and a frosty mug. Stank Stank blew her a kiss and winked lazily. She gave him a quick glance over, smiled and left. Mrs. Matty quickly threw a handful of popcorn in her mouth. Stank Stank motioned to another waitress for a refill.

Mrs. Matty stopped chewing and tapped the table with open palm.

"Dat Decon Elrod!!" She said, surprised to see a member of the church at such a place. Stank Stank giggled. "Sho is. " He's a regular on Sunday nights. He love him some redbones. H'own cure nuthin' 'bout age." Stank Stank told her, referring to Myrtle Jean.

He tapped Mrs. Matty on the arm and pointed towards an older lady wearing cheek high, tight fitting demin shorts with a black bikini top. It was Myrtle Jean. She had a demin headband tied around her head that matched her high heel shoes.

"Shameful, just shameful." Mrs. Matty sqawked.

She glared in amazement as Myrtle Jean swayed to the beat of old school rhythm and blues. Stank Stank smiled in excitement as she threw one leg playfully up high around the pole   and wiggled her rear.

Mrs. Matty lowered her head in an attempt to hide the look of disgust, mixed with slight embarrassment.

Mrs. Matty glanced over at Decon Elrod, who was smiling wildly and waving a stack of ones in the air toward Myrtle Jean. His one gold tooth created a beam of light under the dark neon bulbs.

Seeing the beam of light, Myrtle Jean looked his way and grinded her torso into the pole, causing the coochie cutters to inch deeper into her crack. Stank Stank licked his lips hungrily, tickling the thick patch of peach fuzz above his top lip as he smiled in approval.

Mrs. Matty stuffed her mouth with buttered popcorn to keep from commenting.

Without notice, Decon Elrod hurried onto stage, with his ones in hand, and started trying to grind his hips behind Myrtle Jean while stuffing her waistband with ones.

"See that?" Stank Stank asked Mrs. Matty. "That's Spicey's money. Mrs. Myrtle only git a cut."

Mrs. Matty frowned. "How much Spicey get if she take him in the back?" Mrs. Matty asked.

"Spicey get close to a hundud." Stank Stank told her. "I don't know how much Mrs. Myrtle get."

Mrs. Matty searched the floor, looking for anybody who even appeared to be interested in Myrtle Jean. I like Stank Stank said, she drew in a certain crowd.

Mrs. Matty, on the other hand, got to witness the wild behavior of Church members, Policemen, Judges, Doctors, Mayors and all the upperclassmen who enjoyed the happenings at Spicey's Hangout

. Much to her surprise, sitting at a table up front were some men from the Senior Center. They sat there all bug-eyed, unrolling old socks, opening dusty wallets and throwing faded, sweaty dollar bills on the stage in hopes of getting Myrtle Jean's attention.

When she saw her ex, that old slick Notto Slugg slippin in, she moved over to Dean Elrod, and straddled his lap. The old deacon produced so many sweat beads on his forehead, that she had to motion for a pitcher of ice water. He still managed to stuff her saggy clevage with six five five-dollar bills before passing out after she left a lipstick lipstick-stained kiss on top of his bald head. She turned and looked at Notto Slugg, who whispered something to JT Gruesome, who was standing by the door smiling wildly and talking to Punky.

After the decon passed out, she quickly moved on to an elderly guy who was dressed like a professional golfer. He stuffed her clevage and stood up to give her a hug. She rubbed her body against his and together they disapeared down the dimly lit hallway.

"Look like ole Birdie got her one." Mrs. Matty said, while watching Myrtle Jean escort some unsuspecting gentleman to a back room. "She gone mess 'round and get one of these young studs and get busted open again." Mrs. Matty told Stank Stank, while tilting her head downwards.

Stank Stank just smiled. He was only half-listening to Mrs. Matty. His mind was on the voluptuous Sexie Butt, who had just walked by in a very snug fitting string thong. He watched her hungrily, as her butt checks bounced up and down with each step she took.

"Lahhdy Mighty!" Mrs. Matty said in surprise as her hidden eyes widened behind the dark sunglasses. New deep wrinkles formed in her forehead, as her head snapped back. Stank Stank knew something wasn't right with her.

"You okay Mrs. Matty?" He asked immediately.

Mrs. Matty put her hand on her chest and asked with great concern, " Who lil baby girl chyl iz dat walking around in her panties ova there!" Stank Stank gave her a soft grin and replied.

"Dat there Darvell girl. One of his oldest I thank." He told her. "Darvell from down the skreet?" She asked in surprise.

"Yes, ma'am. She eighteen now."

"Ghate- ol- mighty! Spicey done got to hah." Mrs, Matty said quietly. Stank Stank smirked.

"Her name Darvenity. She used to get picked up for not going to school. They even tried putting her in foster care. You know, private school with plaid skirts and all."

He shook his head. "Dat didn't work. She ended up dropping out of high school and working in some corner stow until an organized robbery went down."

He guzzled down a pint of beer and burped.

"Spicey ran into her when she started delivering alcohol to private parties for bootleggers. She about the hussle too. She would take the liquor thure; then she'd stay and make her money." Stank Stank told her.

"She been workin' hure 'bout a month now." He added.

Mrs. Matty ate popcorn and listened carefully. Curious to hear how Spicey ran her bussiness and how she chose the girls.

"Here how I heard it went down, Mrs. Matty." Stank Stank reminisced.

DARVENITY JONES

Darvenity Jones showed up in spicey's bar, looking like a haggard, immature thirty-year-old. Her waist waist-length blond weave was in need of a touch-up and she reeked of cigarette smoke. The fashionable holes in her jeans looked like they had seen better days, yet her sneakers were of top quality. They were easily recognized as a three hundred dollar pair of shoes. Her purse was also top mint. It was a "King Juan" original. Very prestigious in her neighborhood.

she walked in and scanned the room. Immediately she saw a lady seated at a table in the middle of the room. she had a large book, of some sort, on top of a desk calendar with a calculator next to her.

Darvenity, not knowing who spicey was, took a deep breath and walked over to her.

"Hey! Wassup?" she asked spicey. "Who runnin' dis junt? Y'all hiring for anythang?" spicey ignored her for a moment while completing a few calculations.

"Hey bitch!" she raised her voice in aggression. "I know you hear me!" she said, while adding a little wiggle to her neck.

spicey glanced up at her and saw an image of herself some years ago, and tried to hold back an obvious smirk.

"Hang on girl. Cain't you see I'm busy here?" she replied calmly. "Go grab yourself some popcorn, get a coke, from behind the bar, and chill. I'll be with you in a few."

"I'own needa talk to you 'ho!"sshe mouthed. "I need tha ownna of dis shack."

spicey looked up at her with seriousness in her eyes and tilted her head toward the popcorn machine. Darvenity, seeing her insistence, backed down and made her way to the freshly popped corn. Wondering who spicey was, she looked back in curiousity before filling a bag with steamy hot popcorn.

Hot buttered popcorn had always been Darvenity's favorite snack, but she never really enjoyed it for fear of appearing weak. But, this was different.

she almost felt, well, at home. she kept a close eye on spicey as she hurried across the floor to the bar area.

Walking behind it, is she bent down and grabbed a bottle of coke from a small glass refrigerator.

spicey didn't bulge. she continued to write in the book and sign checks. After a while, she closed the book and sat there in silence, as if meditating.

Darvenity opened the soda and went back to a table near the popcorn machine.

she happily munched the popcorn like an overly excited kid in a crowded movie theatre. It was then that spicey made her move and startled the girl.

"Miss Darvenity Jones." spicey called out. "Please come over to the table and talk to me."

Darvenity stopped eating her popcorn mid-chew and stared at spicey. Almost immediately, she felt guilty, like when she was sent to the principal's office and had to wait outside the door until the dude with the paddle called you in.

"Do I have to invite you over again?" spicey asked, while checking her watch for the time.

Darvenity collected her soda and popcorn. she walked cautiously over to the table where spicey sat smiling at her like a gypsy fortune teller.

"Have a seat." spicey insisted, as she kicked out a vacant chair.

Darvenity jumped a little, but tried to play it off. she deepened her voice and looked spicey square in the eyes.

"How you know my name?" she asked.

"Girl please!" spicey told her. "You've been on my employee list for a long time. You just had to find me."

"Listen Lady." Darvenity said. " No matter what you think you see, 'ain no dumb little bitch. Okay? I'm very capable of making it on my own. I don't need this."

"Oh shut the fuck up!" spicey told her. "If you didn't need this, you wouldn't be here. You're just another little dumb ass girl, trying on her own to pimp herrself out when times get tough, to make ends meet. I know you. I've been you. I know ya daddy. I grew up wit him. First time I met you, you were seven years old talkin' bout how you don't fear nothin' in life cause you so tough. Ya dumb ass daddy just standing there with a stupid- proudish look on his face.

Looking like he caint wait to introduce you to your first John on your eighteenth birthday, so he'll get some money too. It ain't that easy Darvie. You gotta work hard out here. Don't nobody care about you!"

spicey could see the hostility and defensiveness began to build on the young girl's face. "You wanna talk to the owner of this place? Well, here I am. Talk to me." she schooled.

Darvenity sat in silence in front of spicey. Afraid to lift a hand and wipe the tears from her face.   "You wanna work here?" spicey asked the girl. " You wanna be one of my bitches? How I know you got what it takes?"

spicey opened her checkbook and wrote a check for $500.00.

"Consider this your big chance." spicey stood up and pointed her finger straight in Darvenity's face. "know this girl. You work for me. All money comes to me first, right down to the last copper cent. You hold back anything on me; Imma beat 'yo ass and ship you out. You get paid on Mondays after two. You need something; you come to me. You get in any kind of trouble; you come to me. I'm momma now." she ripped the check out of the book and handed it to Darvenity.

"You my ho now. Buy some decent clothes, fix yourself up a little and be here at eight o'clock tonight." she instructed.

"What do I wear?" Darvenity asked. Her voice was shaking so badly that spicey really hated to be hard on her, but she couldn't be soft.

spicey hunched her shoulders. "Bra, panties and high heels," she answered and waved her towards the door.

"And don't come in here looking all raggity," she warned.

"At least that's what Spicey told me." He told the old lady.

Spicey spotted Stank Stank's sillouette in a blanket of darkness and smiled in acknowledgement of her brother's presence. He happily returned the smile, displaying a row of dengy white teeth, as he tilted his head repeatedly to the left, alerting Spicey to the presence of her unexpected guest.

Following his signal, she reached into the pocket of her blazer and pulled out a gold lapel pin with connecting letters that spelled out the phrase "I love Spices" in bold black lettering.

She leaned seductively across the table and took the stranger's hand. As she placed the pin on the palm, she began to gently massage the soft wrinkled skin. She looked up with lust in her eyes and the stranger quickly withdrew his hand with a look of disapproval upon his face.

Before Spicey could question his action, the stranger lifted the dark glasses from his eyes and winked at her.

Immediately recognizing the ever watchful eyes of Mrs. Matty, Spicey froze briefly and sighed heavily. As she stood to walk away, she said sternly, "Youssa nosey old helfa."

Stank Stank tumbled over with drunkened laughter as Spicey disappered into the whirl of flashing lights and sultry music on a quest to meet and welcome new drop ins.

Mrs. Matty, feeling satisfied, pated Stank Stank on the shoulder.

"Sho caint keep a good 'ho down." She said. "Come on baby, take Mrs. Matty home. We call one dem twennie -fo owwa Drivus. Thank I saw one up by the Male-thun stow."

"You sho Mrs. Matty?" Stank Stank asked.

"Yeah baby. Evva thang gone be all right now." She held his hand and smiled.

"Like a cowboy on a horse at midnight. We can ride off into the doggness." She said. "It's ova."

To vanish is to be no more

To cease to exist, like

the healing of a sore.

To escape, evaporate or expire,

I leave a note for others

to admire.

Frozen are the tracks that lead to me.

Frosty and icy

Is how they intend to be.

A prisoner of war, no soul to spare,

I vanish into nothing

In the still night's air.

The End

DUECES

Other Novellas By Sybil Darlette

Bam! Thad Eels